BIG BAD RIVER

Casey only wanted to prove-up his land in the Black Hills. An early round-up netted him a good score of mavericks, but he never finished the trail to Cheyenne. A raid, supposedly by Indians, almost cost him his life, and it was two years before Casey returned to claim his land. Then it was to find it had been stolen by neighbour Corey Lomas and a bunch of hard cases. Casey thought he'd found help, but in the end he had to rely on his own guns and fists and sheer stubbornness to claim what was rightfully his . . .

Books by Tyler Hatch
in the Linford Western Library:

A LAND TO DIE FOR
BUCKSKIN GIRL
DEATHWATCH TRAIL
LONG SHOT
VIGILANTE MARSHAL
FIVE GRAVES WEST

TYLER HATCH

BIG BAD RIVER

Complete and Unabridged

LINFORD
Leicester

First published in Great Britain in 2003 by
Robert Hale Limited
London

First Linford Edition
published 2004
by arrangement with
Robert Hale Limited
London

British Library CIP Data

Hatch, Tyler
Big bad river.—Large print ed.—
Linford western library
1. Western stories
2. Large type books
I. Title
823.9′14 [F]

ISBN 1–84395–579–2

Published by
F. A. Thorpe (Publishing)
Anstey, Leicestershire

Set by Words & Graphics Ltd.
Anstey, Leicestershire
Printed and bound in Great Britain by
T. J. International Ltd., Padstow, Cornwall

This book is printed on acid-free paper

1

'As Good As Dead!'

Casey figured it was a pretty good deal: drive Corey Lomas's cows with his own herd to market at Cheyenne, and keep ten per cent of the selling price.

Not that Lomas was all that great a neighbour back in the Black Hills, but he seemed fair when it came to paying for services rendered. Hard man at times, whipped those men of his along on his spread that abutted against Casey's full section, encompassing river-bottom to timbered hills. *Impatient* was likely the best word to describe Lomas, wanted to go places and at full speed.

Like this trail-drive deal. Didn't want to take time off from building a small dam in his southern pasture so he could boost the grass growth and so fatten his steers for next season.

'I got most of what I need, Case,' he had told Casey when he had first approached him with the deal. 'Men are fellin' trees, got some cee-ment on the siding down at Rapid City and a feller comin' by stage from Deadwood to get me started. I take time for a big trail drive now, I'll miss him — and he's doin' it for a mighty low price, I gotta tell you — and I need someone with know-how . . . Ten per cent of the sellin' price is okay, ain't it?'

Casey agreed it was. 'How many head you want to push in with mine, Corey?'

'Well, boys've done a partial round-up and I'm thinkin' I'll leave the rest up in the brush till next season or grab 'em when winter forces 'em down and keep 'em low till round-up. Reckon I can come up with three hundred, mebbe four at a pinch. You can handle 'em?'

Casey nodded slowly. 'Yeah, that's okay. Won't need to put on any extra men. Leaving Reno here. He's gonna start on my main cabin.'

He had been living in a slapdash clapboard-and-sheet-iron affair this first season so as to pour all his money into cattle. He hoped it would pay off: he had a mighty fine herd ready for the Cheyenne markets where, the word was, the army was paying top price and a premium for good beef.

'That old man?' Lomas had said, frowning. 'You leavin' Reno to build you a *house*? Man, he'll never get it done before next Christmas!'

'I hope like hell I'm back before then. No, he's just making a start, getting the foundations ready. I'll work with the boys to get the timber cut and dressed once we're back.'

Lomas looked thoughtful. 'Just givin' the oldster somethin' to do, huh? Yeah, I can savvy that. Tell you what: I might not know too much about buildin' a dam across the river, but I *can* build cabins. Was with the Pioneer Corps durin' the war. We're gonna have some logs left over from the dam, I reckon.

Sort of like to have too much rather than too little, always been my way. I'll have the boys drag across whatever we don't need at the river and if Reno's got the foundations finished, we'll get 'em laid, ready for when you get back. We'll take care of things for you.'

The offer surprised Casey some because it wasn't like Lomas. It was strictly tit-for-tat with the man; you scratch my back, I scratch yours. Casey wondered what it would cost him eventually in this case — but it was a good offer and he accepted.

Two days later he and five men, including a hardcase named Tripp, as Lomas's representative, started driving the 1400 steers south and west towards distant Cheyenne.

* * *

It was a comfortable run, graze being lush and plentiful, and with water no more than a day's drive between rivers or creeks. They had settled into a routine, working a rotation of nighthawks, and took turns at cooking, and it looked like being a duck-walk all the way down to market.

Then . . .

They had just cleared the foothills of the southern Blacks, near the Wind Caves, when they were hit.

A bunch of riders swept in out of the midnight shadows, a'whooping and a'hollering fit to bust, punctuating the wild Indian-type yells with gunfire. The two nighthawks, Casey's own men, went down dragging at their weapons but never had a chance to fire them.

The raiders swept in in a wide arc, broke into two curved lines, one lot making for the now bawling herd as the cows jumped to their feet and gathered themselves for the inevitable stampede, the other line cutting into the camp as the sleepy trail-men rolled out of their blankets, instinctively snatching shooting-irons.

Casey heard Billy Ketchum gasp, saw the boy's silhouette briefly as he doubled up with the lead smashing into his belly. He swung his own gun at a rider thundering towards him, the man leaning out of the saddle to swipe at him with what looked like a hatchet.

It knocked off his hat and he felt the thud and sting of the turning blade as it just missed cleaving his skull. But it tore away a fair amount of skin and hair and blood flooded down his face. He fired by instinct as he dropped to his knees and went down with the hurtling body of the raider crashing into him. Head buzzing and vision wild, he kicked and thrust to push the man from him and then he saw someone afoot, swinging a rifle towards him.

He triggered, saw the man jerk and stumble, and then the horse with the empty saddle was in front of him and he leapt for it, grabbing the horn with blood-slippery fingers, one boot seeking the dangling stirrup.

Lying across the mount, fighting to work his right leg over, he thought: *This ain't any Indian saddle!* and then he was settled in leather, snatching at the flying reins, ramming home his heels. The horse responded and Casey veered away from the camp. In the glow of the scattered camp-fire, which had set some bedding ablaze, he saw the bodies of his men, Tripp holding his side as he tried to get both legs under him.

Then, unbelieving, he watched the man bring up his sixgun and shoot — *at him*! Casey heard the bullet hit the horse. The animal faltered, then picked up again, stumbling. There was still a lot of yelling and shooting and he veered away from that, followed the bawling of the stampeding steers, but glimpsed the white smear of river-rapids to his left. They had bedded down upstream, at the ford, so he must have come at least a half-mile . . .

But they were still after him. Lead cut random paths in the night and through the roaring in his ears he heard men calling to one another: *white men*!

This was no Indian attack, only white renegades *dressed* as Indians . . .

Then the horse started to go down as a group closed in, guns blazing, flickering muzzle-flashes stabbing the night. Wiping blood out of his eyes, he stood in the stirrups to see how close to the riverbank he was and felt the smashing jar of lead taking him low down in the back.

He grunted involuntarily, feeling a wave of nausea, and was hurled from the saddle as the horse's legs folded under it and he sailed over its head. There was a glimpse of pale, creamy, torn water below as it foamed and frothed and swirled through rocks and water logged trees and then he was in the midst of it.

It closed over his head and poured down his throat. His arms thrashed but — strangely — he couldn't feel if his legs were moving although he willed them to kick like hell.

Then he went under and was sucked down, his body twisted and wrenched and smashed into underwater obstructions as the roaring torrent shot him away into the wildest part of the turbulent water.

On the bank, two horsemen reined down and a third limped up, one arm pressed against his bleeding side as he leaned over to help ease the pain of his wound.

'He — dead?' panted Tripp, gritting his teeth.

'As good as,' answered the nearest rider, tearing off his sweaty feather headband and ripping open his buckskin jacket, revealing pale white skin in both cases. 'Be glad to get outta this Injun outfit.'

'Never mind that!' snapped Tripp hoarsely. 'I gotta know about Casey!'

'Relax,' said the second rider harshly. 'He's dead. Like the rest of his outfit . . . '

'Better had be,' Tripp said. 'Gimme a leg up and ride me back to my own mount. We got us some roundin'-up to do come daylight.'

* * *

They were a group of Black Hills Sioux, related to the Oglallas, and they were in the process of breaking camp, preparing to move on from this gravel-spit that projected into the wild river. White men's maps called it the Big Cheyenne, although the name was often spoken as Big Bad River, for it was unpredictable and roaring floods surged out of the hills, with snow-melt and heavy rains turning it into a destructive force. The Shadow Men who had come here long ago, long before the whites, in their shining metal clothes, bringing horses that were unknown to the people of the Great Plains before this, called the river *Pasado*. A long time later they had come to know this meant 'bad', in reference mostly to food and meat, although it could be applied to water. Perhaps the white men also knew this and that was why they called it Big Bad River amongst themselves.

But the tribe knew it as the River-of-Anger-and-Peace, turbulent waters of volatile moods, benign beneficiary as well as violent killer of men.

This far downstream the waters were wide and shallow and peaceful, only swirling here and there with pools of current in against the rocks, lapping in small waves on the gravel beach.

They were loading the canoes when Eyes-Like-Hawk called, pointing, and it took them several seconds to see what he had seen in a flash: a humped, rolling form breaking the water on the far side of the beach, flopping in an awkward movement as legs trailed in the edge of a current.

A man.

White man, they soon discovered, dragging out the body with the bloody head-gash, other wounds showing: one low down in the back which hadn't bled much, another beneath a shoulder. The left arm flopped, obviously broken. The battered man's once fair hair was plastered with gravel and blood to his rugged white face but there was no sign of life.

'Give him to the river,' grunted Blue Ear.

'He lives!' cried Fat Deer, her braids swinging as she grabbed the torn shirt and heaved the white man up on to the gravel. 'He still lives!'

The others, turning away to continue breaking camp paused only briefly.

'Not for long,' said Blue Ear, spitting disdainfully: he had no use for white men, alive or dead.

'We cannot leave him!' cried a middle-aged woman with grey-shot hair, running to kneel beside the white man, pushing his hair back from his face. Her dark eyes were bright as she looked up into the rugged, unsmiling face of Blue Ear. 'It is he! The One!'

Her words brought a startled murmur from the people and they all crowded out on to the gravel beach, staring down at the sprawled, barely-living white man.

The middle-aged woman, Silver Top, clawed at Blue Ear's buckskins, nodding emphatically. 'There is no mistake. He is The One!'

The tall warrior felt all eyes upon him but he would not look down at the white man. He stared over the heads of the others, downriver, thinking of their next camp, and what it would mean to have a white man on the edge of death there for weeks, perhaps months, while they worked to bring him back from the Dark World.

But, if Silver Top was right — and his heart told him she was — it must be done.

'Prepare him for the river journey,' he said gutturally, and strode away from the group.

2

Long Recovery

He thought he recognized the leather-faced squaw with the silver streaks in her hair but he couldn't recall her name. He had seen her somewhere before, though, but darned if he could recall where, or who she was.

Then the biggest shock came when he realized he couldn't remember his *own* name!

He had never felt such fear knotting his belly, making his brain reel, constricting his throat. Silver Top saw his writhings beneath the buffalo robes and thought he was in fever again, pulled away some of the robes. Then she saw his face and the terror in his pale-blue eyes staring up at her and she knew something was wrong. Something bad.

'You — safe,' she told him in halting English. She patted the pile of animal hides he was lying on. 'Here. Safe for you. Me — I am friend. You — help me — five summers, long time ago.'

He frowned, still staring. Her words meant nothing to him. Oh, he understood their meaning but he did not recall her or savvy what she was telling him. She elaborated in her slow English, telling how seven white soldiers had attacked their hunting village while the men were away. Killed the other five women and all the children, scalped most of them. Then Casey showed up. She was hurt, could use only one arm, trying to bury the pitiful remains of the children. He had been running a trapline, it seemed, for he had a mule laden with animal pelts.

He tended her wounds, buried the children with tenderness, self-consciously said a Christian prayer over them, made wooden crosses. She was afraid of him at first, then recognized something decent in his face, not like the madness and lasciviousness of the soldier troop. He made shelter for her and went away, came back two nights later, wounded and bloody, not speaking about what had happened.

Then he took her to the edge of her tribal country, within sight of her home village at the Green Bend of the river . . .

'You ride away again,' she finished. 'I — not see you till — here?'

'Now,' he corrected quietly, still frowning, remembering nothing of what she said.

'You kind to me — save life — and, later, warriors find seven white soldiers with some of our scalps — all dead, shot. They find your tracks — make them gone . . . '

'You're saying I went after the soldiers who wiped out your camp and — killed 'em?'

'Sign say so. We look long for you.'

Hope surged in him and his hand clawed at her so suddenly that she jumped. 'My name! You know my name?'

Frowning, she shook her head. 'We call you 'The One' . . . The One Who Helps . . . '

His shoulders sagged in disappointment and he winced at the pain beneath his left shoulder. He tried to ease his body around to a more comfortable position, learned that his left arm was splinted and slung in a length of rawhide.

But his face, grey and pain-etched, suddenly looked haunted as he stared into her eyes. She dropped her gaze. She could barely hear him as he said,

'I — can't — move — my legs!' Breath exploded from him as realization slammed home like a kick from a mustang. She heard his next words because he yelled them: '*Jesus, Mary and Joseph — I can't — move my — goddamn — legs!*'

Her hand pushed against his chest, holding him down with surprisingly little effort.

'I — sorry. You can not — walk . . . Never.'

He fell away into unconsciousness, his fevered mind finding this too much to handle.

* * *

Casey had been with the Indians for three weeks now and he still didn't know who he was. Blue Ear — no friend to any white man, though reluctantly beholden to Casey for what he had done for Silver Hair and the tribe's dead children — travelled far to try to find out his identity.

The warrior, chief of this small breakaway band of the Black Hills Sioux, came to the conclusion that Casey, now known as 'The Strange One' among his people, had been wounded way upriver from where they had found his body. Blue Ear learned there had been a battle with renegade Indians raiding a trail herd bound for Cheyenne.

'Maybe your cows,' he told Casey as the morose man sat propped up on a framework of saplings covered with animal skins for padding.

'Means nothing to me,' Casey said and he sounded ungrateful, for deep down he was angry at the world and everyone in it for dealing him such a blow as this. Not only no memory of his previous life, but no damn legs to walk on so he could even try to find out who the hell he was once he was better . . . Better! . . . That was a laugh! Sure, his arm and shoulder might mend, but not his legs! How could a man hope to get better when he would not be able to walk ever again . . .

But another week and Silver Top and a young squaw — her daughter he suspected — named Sweet Sage, carried his frame seat to the edge of the river and without ceremony, tilted it up and dumped him in the shallows. They stood on the bank with other women and hooting youths and laughing children, amused as he floundered and splashed, fit to be tied.

He pounded the shallows in frustrated anger, gasping as river water ran down his face, nearly blinding him. 'Damn you all!' he gritted. 'Always knew Injuns had a warped sense of humour! This — ain't — funny! Goddamnit, I — can't — *walk*! Can't you savvy that! I — have — to — *walk*!

Silver and Sage waded in, took him by the loose folds of the buckskin shirt he now wore and dragged him into deeper water. He began to panic, not knowing what they were about, and he struck out at them, blindly and wildly, missing every time. They turned him face down and he gulped and spat and retched the brown water.

He knew they were doing something to his legs but couldn't tell what because he had so little feeling — hardly any — below the waist. Twisting his upper body, he found that each woman held one leg and worked them as they were supported by the water in a pumping motion that resembled a walking action.

'What the hell you doing?' he demanded.

'You want walk,' Silver told him, 'you — work.'

'How the hell can I work at it when I can't even move my goddamn legs, you — you blamed idiots!'

Sage, young and blooming, smiled at him with white perfect teeth, raven hair glinting in the high mountain sun.

'We make legs walk for you,' she told him with a hint of laughter. 'You lazy, no strong. We help — you help, too. Or not walk at all.'

He glared, but began to calm down, his upper body moving with their efforts. After a while he could find a rhythm there and began to anticipate it, moving what muscles he could as they worked his legs.

But his black mood returned when they dragged him out on to the bank where he lay, letting his buckskins dry in the sun. He tried to move his legs himself. There was absolutely no response, not even a twitch.

'You're wasting your time,' he snapped as Silver knelt beside him. She began to knead the muscles in his thigh, Sage working on his calf muscles.

'We — try,' the older woman panted. 'We try — long time. But bullet still in your back.'

He stiffened. 'The bullet's still in there? Where?'

She touched his lower spine but he felt nothing.

'Can you see it?'

'Hole nearly — nearly close over,' Sage told him.

'But — can — you see — the damn — bullet!'

'See it — yes.'

Gasping a little, he lay back, thinking about this. By next morning he knew what had to be done. The bullet was obviously pressing against some spinal nerve that was cutting off his ability to move his legs. The solution seemed simple enough to him: remove the bullet and free the nerve, and he would walk again.

But after further thought he wasn't so sure. He had been wounded at Gettysburg, spent a long time in various field hospitals, seeing the crude surgery and watching many men die who might have lived in a civilian hospital. When he was classed as 'walking wounded' he had helped the doctors, watched operations, even done some comparatively simple ones himself, such as taking Rebel musket balls out of arms and legs and easily reached body parts. He remembered one that a doctor had stopped him from attempting to remove.

'Son, that ball's too close to the spine. You slip and the man's paralysed for life. It's best left alone, may even work itself out in time . . . '

He grew excited. *He was remembering!* Not realizing that amnesia can be selective, recalling things from a man's earliest years, yet not allowing him to remember what he had for breakfast or where he slept the night before . . .

But that wasn't important right now.

He had to walk again! *Had to*! Even if he didn't know who he was, if he could walk he could travel and would eventually find out.

But that bullet — if it wasn't removed properly, then he would be paralysed forever.

⋆ ⋆ ⋆

It took him two more days before he worked up enough courage to take a chance and agree to an attempt to remove the bullet. Silver said she would try, and consulted the local shaman who chanted over him and used sacred eagle-feathers to drift smoke from the holy fire into his nostrils. Maybe there was some sort of weed or herb in it for it smelled funny and he felt drugged afterwards, had only a hazy idea of what was going on around him.

At first he did not feel Silver's probing and then, suddenly, there was excruciating, knifing pain in his lower back that tore a scream from him. He slumped and fell into oblivion.

* * *

He awoke in agony, but he didn't care, surprised the Indian audience by actually laughing, even as his teeth drew blood from his lower lip. The pain was damn near intolerable — but it was *below waist level, running down both legs*!

This he could endure, standing on his head playing a set of bagpipes if any happened to be handy, or any other way necessary. His nerves were working again, and while his legs still wouldn't move just because he willed them to, it was a start, a start that engendered hope and finally pushed aside his black moods of despair.

The sessions in the river with the women working his legs and afterwards massaging his muscles were now fun, filled with more laughter than curses. The kids of the village came and took turns at kneading his legs, their small fingers tickling, making him writhe — which he saw as another good sign.

Headaches were still with him and there was fog cramming his skull when he tried to remember who he was and how he had been wounded. The head wound had healed but a section of scalp and hair the size of his palm had been removed. He would simply let his hair grow long and hang down to cover the bald patch, he decided.

The shaman came and lit his secret fires, sprinkled them with strange dusts, chanted his spells, hung crystal-like stones around Casey's neck, even bound some against the wound site on his spine and the one on the side of his head. Nothing did any good but they were trying to help and he did not complain.

Six weeks after Silver and Sage had dumped him in the river, he managed to wiggle one toe.

Three weeks later he was wiggling all the toes of his left foot.

The snows came. Near the tribe's winter camp there were hot sulphur springs. He was taken there daily, immersed in the hot water, his skin glowing and burning, feeling as if it would slough off his bones, and then he was buried to the waist in snow, upper body actually turning blue with the cold. Sage and Silver only laughed.

He accused the women of taking advantage of him.

During this time, Blue Ear brought him a bundle wrapped in rawhide. When he unrolled it, he found a Sharps Big Fifty rifle with the falling-block action and a Vernier-scale peep sight. Only thing was, it was in a couple of dozen pieces.

By now he could speak a little Sioux and he had taught Silver and Sage to speak English more fluently. He learned that there was once a buffalo hunter named Bighead Jack who roamed as far north as the Musselshell and who traded pelts and brought the tribe buffalo-meat in the winter. He had died, frozen to death, and they had found this rifle package beside him, no other firearms, not even his skinning knife.

'Someone found him before you did, I'd figure, took his guns, didn't know enough to try to assemble this Sharps so left it with him . . . '

'You fix gun?' asked Blue Ear who had thawed some over the months Casey had been in the camp.

'Might be able to. There's a broken file here, a pair of pliers and a wrench. Can use some of your bear-grease for lubrication — but what about ammo? Bullets?'

Blue Ear hesitated, then reached under his jacket and brought out a crumpled and stained cardboard box. It held a dozen cigar-sized .50 calibre cartridges, the brass greenish, the lead hand-moulded, with the tips cut crosswise for quick expansion. 'Have more box.' He held up five fingers.

Casey grinned; at last he had something he could really get his teeth into, instead of doing women's work, shucking corn, rubbing buckskin, gathering firewood — being pulled along on a sled by laughing gangs of Indian kids. Now he had something he could concentrate on — a white-man thing. But some of the edge of his new excitement dulled as he remembered that — he *couldn't* remember!

⋆ ⋆ ⋆

There were still buffalo in some of the canyons, pawing through the covering of frost and snow, finding enough grass to eat. And Casey didn't need to walk to hunt.

They took him to where he wanted to go on one of their sleds with antler runners, laid out a thick buffalo-hide for him to stretch out on, and then he told them where to hammer in the forked stick. They helped him with the heavy, cumbersome Sharps rifle, rested the barrel in the fork and made him comfortable, propping rolled and folded hides under his hips or side as he directed them to, steadying his body.

There were about forty buffalo down in the canyon, happily grazing, winter hides glistening thick and warm under the dusting of fresh snow. He searched for and found the lead bull, blue steam jetting from the flaring nostrils as he rummaged, grumbling deep. Casey settled his cheek against the cold smooth wood of the stock, smelled the bear-grease he had used to lubricate the new parts he had made and on the action itself.

He opened the breech smoothly and silently, slid in one of the huge cartridges, closed the action and squinted through the peep sight. When the Sharps fired, he felt the belting jolt in his lower back, the area of the wound. *And* — he wasn't quite sure — it seemed to him the rippling concussion ran down *both* legs, clear to his toes!

But he had no time to think about it. The big bull was down on its knees, snorting, blood now jetting from its nostrils, and he knew his bullet had torn up the lungs. It stayed there, expiring with heavy rhythmic grunts, some of the cows nearby lifting heads curiously for a moment or two, before continuing to chew and forage, unconcerned.

The next report seemed even louder to Casey. His nostrils twitched with the bite of burning gunpowder and another animal collapsed, thrashing briefly. Blue Ear, stretched out alongside Casey, grinned despite himself: this was the kind of white man he could grow to like!

Only a few of the herd paused to sniff the breeze and the slight tang of gunsmoke that might have reached down into the canyon, then they lowered their shaggy heads and went on eating.

'Dumb beasts!' Casey remarked and he brought down number three.

'Much blood,' Blue Ear said and Casey nodded a little grimly.

'Yeah, that one sure bled. Must've hit an artery.' If there was too much blood and the herd got the scent they would run.

It happened — but not until he had downed eighteen beasts, and even then he brought down another as he fired into the cloud of snow and earth-clods tossed up by the stampede. Blue Ear and his waiting men were grinning ear to ear.

Casey, exhausted now, shoulder bruised, upper body one huge ache, stretched out on his hides and watched as the Indians started skinning. They had seen the white man's impatient way and, as dark, threatening clouds were hanging on the peaks and sliding rapidly down towards them, they used the same method: simple, bloody and effective.

Cuts were made along the inside of each leg and around the neck after the belly was slit from throat to anus. The heavy skin of the neck — almost an inch thick and much favoured for shields that were said to be able to turn a bullet from a Winchester — was bunched up, wound round with a plaited grass rope, the other end twisted around some part of the wooden saddle frame on the waiting mustang. At a signal, the rider raced away, was pulled up short as the rope tightened, the mustang still straining, and suddenly the hide began to rip free of the carcass, revealing the thick layer of white marbled fat and raw red meat. The sucking, crackling sounds came more rapidly until, finally, the hide was free, soggy and dripping, the flayed carcass steaming.

* * *

That night there was a big celebration with much dancing and chanting and everyone gorged on buffalo meat. The women scraped and pegged and salted the hides or chewed them soft for making robes and wrap-arounds for the *papooses*.

Casey enjoyed himself despite his inability to move around much: he was able to hobble a little now, held up by a strong warrior on each side, feet dragging or flopping in a caricature of walking. Strangely, this accomplishment only depressed him: he had never been one to depend on others.

Over the next few weeks he showed the men how to use the Sharps and there were many sore shoulders and loosened teeth and much wailing on behalf of the wild 'warriors' but by then the buffalo had scattered, moved on to some other winter refuge. But the men who had learned how to control the heavy Sharps brought back wolfskins and elk and whitetail deer and tender venison was often on the menu.

Sage had long since moved into his bed and he had learned, under her expert touch, that he had not lost *all* feeling below the waist after all. He was well fed and waited on by eager squaws and the warriors seemed to have a high regard for him.

He should have been happy enough — at least he was still alive. *But he still didn't know who he was!*

The warriors boasted of battles they had been in, youths told of wild romantic conquests that were pure fantasy and urged him to match their tales. He tried, using his imagination, and found that he was able to bring back actual details he had previously forgotten. Not many, and he couldn't be sure if they were fact or fantasy, but perhaps this was a good sign, the effort awakening a thought process in him that had long been disused.

Then one night he woke sweating, heart pounding, with a rapidly fading memory of a ranch house with an old grey-bearded man standing in the doorway. He groaned aloud as he made an effort to hold the details — but lost them all too quickly.

'I — almost had it! — I *know* that ranch was mine!'

Sage studied him soberly with large brown eyes.

His legs slowly improved and by winter's end he was using crutches made from forked saplings to drag himself around the camp. His headaches were back and he had many dreams but always lost the memory of them almost at the moment he awoke.

They were always about a ranch, set in high, heavily timbered mountains. Occasionally he saw the grey-bearded man, but mostly it was just the country and sometimes cattle and unidentifiable riders working them.

When summer came and he was getting around without the aid of crutches or stick, stumbling occasionally, he began to ride a horse again. It was wonderful, this new-found freedom that allowed him to explore the country. He had figured out from what Blue Ear and Silver had told him that they were hundreds of miles from the river where they had found him, the nomadic tribe moving in a long-established pattern. Soon after, flashes of real memory began.

He saw the children's bodies scattered amongst the smouldering ruins of the Indian camp, the dead and scalped women, Silver crouching, awkwardly fitting a beaded moccasin to the almost severed foot of a dead girl-child, who had also been scalped.

His heart hammered and bounced against his ribs day after day as he strove to bring back more and more details of each remembered incident. He found the trick was to hold a single event, work on it, recall as much detail as possible, and try to make that particular memory as complete as possible. Next time he recalled something, he went through the same routine, until one hot midsummer night he sat up in bed, quite calmly, touched Sage's warm, naked shoulder and whispered to her.

'My name's Casey — Jackson Howard Casey. But everyone just calls me Casey or Case. I have a ranch in the Black Hills, north of Rapid City, called the J Bar C and I was driving my herd to Cheyenne when we were attacked by white renegades dressed as Indians — I was shot in the back by a man named

Tripp and fell into the Big Bad River and your people pulled me out . . . '

He felt the long smooth length of her supple body suddenly go rigid.

'I am both happy and sad. You are no longer the Strange One. You are — Casey. And you have a ranch and it is in the white man's world — and — and you will go back to this place.'

In the dull smoky light inside the tipi, the bottom hides rolled up to allow cool night air to flow inside, he saw the glisten of tracking tears across her high-boned cheeks.

He sought her hand but she drew it away from him and he nodded and said slowly,

'Yes, Sage — I will be going back.'

But he wondered, after all this time — over a year and a half now — if there was anything for him to go back to.

3

Long Trail Back

Leaving wasn't as easy as he had reckoned.

He was surprised to find he wasn't ready. Riding took it out of him and he found his legs still stiff and awkward. He also had no firearms or weapons of any kind except a knife in a beaded sheath that Blue Ear's youngest son, Stone Man, made for him and presented to him after he had shot the buffalo with the Sharps.

There was little ammunition left for the big rifle and he didn't want to take it with him, in any case: the tribe could use it well and even if the bullets ran out they would find ways of getting more. He had tried shooting the short flatbows the Indians used, carrying them unstrung in a rawhide quiver with arrows behind their wooden saddles, but he did not make a success of it. Stone Man had taken him hunting and he had missed every shot, the arrows either going over or under or even passing behind the animal.

Well, weapons weren't his first priority: getting fit for the long journey was.

It took him another two weeks and by then the tribe was on the move, to the south and west. The direction suited him so he went along until they reached their destination, a campsite in a long canyon by an unnamed river, backed with the cool green of heavy timber, conifers, pitch-pine, balsam fir, larch and cedars. The air was heavy yet sharp with piney scents and it was a pleasant place, full of birdsong.

Casey knew this was his departure point.

Saying farewell wasn't the easiest thing he had ever done, especially to Sage who tried to act casually. He figured she had prepared herself for this moment, knowing all along that, once he could walk again, he would eventually return to the white man's world. He had nothing to give her as a parting gift, so he picked a small bunch of wildflowers and presented them to her, wrapped around with a strip of buckskin on which the shaman had painted totems of good fortune. The tears sprang to her eyes as she clutched the flowers against her breast.

'These I will dry and make a small bag out of the buckskin to carry them near to my heart, Caysee,' she told him. She lowered her eyes and her voice as she added, 'I will use them to tell our son about his father.'

Casey felt an electric shock go through him. 'Son?'

She smiled shyly, rested his hand against her abdomen. 'Sometime in winter he will taste life's first breath. He will be called Walks Tall, after you.'

'Lucky to be walking at all,' he murmured, still off-balance by this news. *My God! A child — his child!* He wasn't quite ready for *that!* And yet . . .

Then Blue Ear handed him the misshapen lead bullet Silver had taken from his back. It had been drilled through and strung on a length of string made from hair — Blue Ear's, some from Silver — the pale strands — and some from Sage.

'Bullet not all bad. It give us you for many moons, Cay-see. You wear — you not forget us.'

'That I will never do,' Casey told him huskily as Sage tied the thong around his neck. The small, unaccustomed weight felt strange and he fingered it as he took his last farewells of Silver and all the others who had come to see him off. He touched Sage's cheek gently before mounting.

He rode out on his mustang, a paint with a mottled nose, lifting a hand as he passed the silent lines of Indians until only the long canyon — and a much longer journey — lay ahead of him.

* * *

Amongst the food in the soft buckskin bag Sage had given him he found a small drawstring poke. When he looked inside, he found some irregular nuggets of gold, small but heavy.

He smiled thinly. He had amused himself at one of the camps panning in the shallows and won only a few flakes of gold. It was of little or no interest to the Sioux but he had mentioned it would buy many things in a white man's town. Where she had got the gold he didn't know but it would sure come in handy. He had enough grub to see him through to a trading post or outlying town and he would buy some sort of gun, then he could live off the land during his long journey south.

And every step of the way he knew he would be thinking about Sage and their unborn son: she insisted it *would* be a boy-child. It was something he didn't know how he felt about and it scared him a little, so that he tried to push it to the back of his mind, concentrate on getting back to his ranch in the Black

Hills, wondering if old Reno was still there.

If the *ranch* was still there!

* * *

It was in a town called Newbo, in the high reaches of the Belle Fourche River and close to what would be later judged as being the geographical centre of the United States, that he found Tripp.

This was sparsely settled country and so attracted men on the dodge or those who simply needed space between them and the law while they went about some lawless deed.

Casey had been travelling for ten days, pushing his paint to the limit, taking advantage of good weather while it lasted. It was growing steadily warmer as he went south and he swung away from the direct trail towards the big lake, figuring the horse would appreciate a swim as much as he would himself. Silver had impressed upon him that he must keep his leg muscles working, build them up to strength. The best way to do this was by walking or swimming. Casey had never been much on swimming, just did enough so he didn't forget how. It had pulled him out of trouble more than once: during the war on a night-time raid across a river that doubled in size and strength of current from a flash flood while they hit the Rebel camp; three times when driving cattle across water . . .

Both animal and man enjoyed a short spell in the cool though unclear water of the lake and then he headed out, decided to stop in Newbo for some tobacco and whatever else the last of his nuggets would buy him. A week ago he had stopped at a place called Owl Bridge in the Little Missouri Breaks and had purchased a second-hand — maybe *twenty*-second-hand, he thought when he took it apart — Winchester '66 in .44 calibre. The trader threw in five boxes of shells and seemed happy with the deal.

Casey worked on the weapon by the

light of his camp-fires, got it in working order, but it threw bullets all over the damn countryside when he came to shoot it. The blade foresight was badly bent, in fact, had a piece of metal broken off completely. In the end he shaped another with his knife-blade from a length of deer-antler he had picked up. It took a little patience to whittle down the blade but he got it just right in the end, and had the added advantage that the white bone foresight was better to shoot with in bad light.

He had the tubular magazine fully loaded with eleven shells when he dismounted outside a ramshackle saloon on Newbo's main drag, carrying the rifle in his right hand as he pushed through the batwings under the silent, unfriendly stares of a group of ragged men sitting on the steps leading up from the muddy gutter.

The bar room smelled bad and was full of shadows, some that moved furtively. Several men were drinking at the bar. There was no mirror — well, just a few jagged shards remaining in a bullet-pocked frame — so they had to turn their heads to see who had entercd. No one showed undue interest in him although a couple stiffened when they saw the rifle. He pulled out a small, pea-sized nugget from the pocket of his buckskin shirt and showed it to the squinting barkeep.

'Will that buy me a beer and some grub?'

The barkeep drew the nugget closer to his cocked eyes, moved to the end of the counter where murky light seeped in through the dirty window glass. He sniffed.

'Two beers an' a plate of grub. Stew today.'

'What's in it?' Casey asked.

The barkeep shrugged. 'Best not to ask. Lots of spice, though, makes it easier to choke down.'

Casey half-smiled despite himself. 'Reckon I'll risk it, but pour me a beer first.'

The barkeep was putting the glass

down in front of him, slopping it over the rim, of course, when Casey heard a chair overturn behind him and a man exclaim, 'Christ! It cain't be!'

Not a voice he remembered, and he didn't even know if the remark was about him, but he turned casually, and looked across a table crammed with plates containing food remnants, dirty glasses, two empty bottles, a greasy pack of scattered cards, and a glass jar of dirty-looking yellow liquid which he guessed passed for the local red-eye.

But it was the man who had risen half out of his chair who interested Casey: beard-shadowed, clothes ragged and trail-stained, hat pushed to the back of a head of shaggy hair, mouth still half-open.

'Tripp! You back-shooting son of a bitch!'

That was all it took to throw the room into chaos. Men who had been at the table with Tripp suddenly deserted like a handful of dead leaves blown by a winter wind, diving for the floor or running for cover at the end of the bar. *Their* movements sent others across the room hunting cover — and with good reason.

Tripp heaved over the table with his left hand, snatched his sixgun with his right and blasted two fast shots in Casey's direction as he turned and streaked for the batwings.

Casey knew he would never catch the man on foot — his legs still weren't that good — so the only way was to stop Tripp in his tracks.

The rifle came in line with his hip, left hand holding the fore end as his right levered and triggered. The crash of the shot rattled a few glasses on the bar shelf and Tripp yelled as his right leg was kicked from under him and he plunged towards the batwings with outstretched hands. His smoking gun punched through the slats on one side and hung up before dropping from his grip. His head hit the other door hard and he spilled on to the boardwalk, scattering the bunch of hardcases who had been sitting there. He grabbed at his wounded leg, rolling about, teeth bared as he cursed in agony.

By then Casey was standing over him, poking the powder-reeking muzzle of the rifle into the man's face. No one interfered — they weren't that kind. If Tripp had trouble, let him get out of it if he could. If he couldn't — well, it was no skin off their noses.

'What'd you do with my herd, you wide-looping bastard.'

Anyone within earshot could tell Casey was riled and ready to blow Tripp's head off if he didn't get the right answers.

Tripp knew it, too, but foolishly tried to bluff his way out.

'Dunno what you're talkin' about. Who the hell are you, anyway?'

Casey kicked him hard on the bleeding leg and Tripp convulsed, yelling and writhing.

'You recognized me inside,' Casey said and a couple of onlookers nodded: that was the truth. 'Thought you'd killed me when you back-shot me and I fell into the river, eh?'

Pale now, short of breath, Tripp stared up at him, decided not to pretend any longer. 'Aw, that night we was hit by Injuns . . . ? Hell, man, it was *wild*! Everyone was shootin' at anythin' that moved. If one of my slugs hit you — an' damned if I know how you could tell *that* — I'm mighty sorry! I was shootin' at fellers I figured for rustlers. Hell, it's close to — what? Two year now. Where the hell you been?'

Casey ignored the question. 'You're a goddamn liar,' he said flatly and there was a sharp intaking of breath from the audience.

Tripp swallowed, licking his dry lips. 'Gimme a break, will you? I was lucky to get outta that raid alive . . . '

Casey kicked him again, harder, and Tripp passed out for a short time. When he came round, he was still looking up the black tunnel of Casey's rifle barrel.

'There's no law here, Tripp, and I reckon you don't have any pards, either.

You're on your own. Just you and me. Now you tell me about that raid on my herd or you're gonna have *two* busted legs and maybe only one ear, or nine toes, or — you savvy?'

Tripp swallowed again, nodded slightly. 'I — I dunno what to say — Injuns come outta nowhere at that night camp and — '

'They were white renegades. Friends of yours. I recollect hearing you talking to 'em — ' Casey thumbed back the hammer of the rifle and Tripp's face began to crumple.

'Wait! Okay. Lomas sent me along to keep an eye on his cows. I had some — friends — in the area. It seemed like too good a chance to let go by.'

Casey spoke slowly, quietly, voice full of menace. 'So the idea was to kill me and my men, take the herd and sell it off cheap to some damn rancher who wouldn't look at the brands too close or ask for a bill of sale.'

Tripp said nothing. The rifle barrel moved in a short arc, opened up his left cheek, knocking him sideways.

'That it, Tripp?'

The man hesitated and then nodded but there was something about the way he looked that puzzled Casey. Almost as if the man had snatched at the explanation, seeing it as a way to get off the hook. Which would mean that Casey had figured it wrong. But what other way was there . . . ?

'Where'd you sell 'em?' he asked suddenly.

Tripp shrugged. 'Like you said, to anyone who didn't want to see a bill of sale. Scattered 'em to hell an' gone all over that territory, took a few weeks. Trouble was, the money only come in in small lots. No one up there was rich enough — or stupid enough — to buy the lot in one hit. We busted up and went our own ways.'

Casey wasn't sure whether to believe the man: it had a ring of truth to it, now, but there was still the way Tripp had grabbed for that explanation . . .

'What about Corey Lomas?'

Tripp arched his eyebrows. 'What about him?'

'You didn't go back to the Black Hills?'

'The hell for? He'd have shot me where I stood if I told him I'd lost his cows to rustlers. Anyway, I'd had enough of ranchin', figured on some easy money and makin' time to live it up a little.'

Casey ran his cold gaze over the dishevelled man. 'See you made it.'

Tripp scowled but said nothing for a moment, a man still in pain but with a lot more confidence now. 'I got no money. Can't pay you back.'

'Figured that I can string you up, Tripp. Rustling, killing — be within my rights.'

Tripp lost his confident look. The words caused a stir among the watchers but Casey knew no one would bother to stop him hanging scum like Tripp.

'Listen!' the wounded man said suddenly, a hint of desperation in his voice. 'I know you're tough, Casey, everyone knows it. But I'll do a deal with you.'

'What the hell kinda deal can you do?' Casey snapped. 'You murdered my men, stole my cattle, left me crippled for nigh on a year. One way or another, you're gonna pay for that, Tripp.'

Tripp's chest was heaving wildly now. 'You gotta listen! It — it might not've been just like you said.'

Casey frowned. 'Then tell me how it was,' he said softly, eyes steady and bleak on Tripp's face.

He could see that Tripp was reluctant but the man was badly scared now, knew there was no help he could call on, and so, like a lot of others who had no code other than taking care of Number One, he turned traitor.

'The — raid on the herd was all arranged,' Tripp croaked eventually. 'Before we left the hills.'

Casey stiffened, frowned, startled. 'You had it fixed with your pards even then?'

Tripp shook his head. 'Not me

— Corey Lomas.'

Casey felt something chill surging through him, something that momentarily froze all thought and movement. Before he could speak, Tripp smiled crookedly, aware of the shock of his words.

'Why you think he only put in a few hundred head? Not that he had many more. He lost a lot of mavericks to your men and he weren't happy about that.'

'I started rounding 'em up earlier and kept at it harder. Corey knows it's the only way of getting a good count of mavericks. If he didn't work his men hard enough, he's a fool.'

'Mebbe. But this dam had him tied up some and — well, other interests . . . But he reckoned it this way: you'd be pushing most of your herd to Cheyenne, and he needed a lot more money for the dam than he could get for sellin' a few cows. So — he put a minimum lot of cows with your herd, offers you ten per cent of the sellin' price — '

'I figured all along it was a mite too generous.' Casey was thinking aloud now.

'Well, he reckoned if he fixed it to rustle the whole shebang and sold 'em off in Cheyenne, he ought to have all the *dinero* he needed.'

'Knowing he'd have to kill me in the process, or I'd find a way of going after my herd — and maybe figuring out what was going on.'

'Yeah, he was mighty leery of you. Knew you had a tough rep and could be a mean son of a bitch if you wanted to.'

Casey shook his head slowly. He had never liked Lomas much, thought the man was land-hungry and didn't treat folk right, but he hadn't picked him to pull something like this.

'And you had to make sure I was killed.'

Tripp didn't want to answer that one. 'It — it was all Corey's plan. I just done what I was paid for.'

'So . . . ? *Did* you sell the herd and so on?'

Tripp hesitated, nodded. 'In Cheyenne. Got top dollar. We had all your papers, no one asked questions when I said I was your ramrod makin' the drive for you.'

'You took the money back to Lomas?'

'Well — mebbe not as much as we got,' Tripp admitted slowly. 'Corey's a bit of a piker, you know. Don't pay all that well . . . '

Looking down at the man's present state, a saddle tramp without a saddle right now, Casey said, 'Why'd he fire you? Find out you'd tried to cheat him?'

'Yeah. I — I was lucky to get out with my neck in one piece. That Durango he has as a kinda bodyguard come after me, but I had some luck when a cougar tore his hoss out from under him. I — ain't done so good since.'

'But you managed to stay alive — till now, leastways.'

'Hey! We got a deal!'

Casey stared silently.

'Goddamnit, we got a deal!'

Casey flicked his gaze around the watching men. 'You hear me agree to any kinda deal with this snake?'

A couple shook their heads, most just stared back or turned away, but it was plain Tripp had no support.

'Aw. Wh- what you gonna do?'

'You're alive — four of my men are dead and I've lost a lot of money. Anyone got a rope I can borrow?'

That even brought a few laughs and one man started towards a tethered horse to get a coiled lariat from his saddle horn — hell, a lynching was as good entertainment as any, except for maybe a young whore learning the trade.

Tripp grabbed at Casey's buckskin trousers, looking up at him, wild-eyed.

'Somethin' else. You need to know this. I — I was holdin' out in case I needed it and I reckon I do now . . . '

Casey had suspected the man wasn't telling the full story. 'Well . . . ?'

'You won't string me up?'

'Depends on what you got to say.'

'Aw, man! Don't be so goddamn — *hard*! All right — I'll take a chance but I know you'll thank me. It's this: Lomas din' only want your herds, he wanted you dead so he could grab your spread! Give him the whole blamed mountain then, as well as the river-bottoms . . . ' Tripp suddenly pulled a wry smile despite his pain. 'That got to you, huh? Sure it did! You're goin' back to nothin', Casey. 'Less it's a grave!'

Tripp was right: the news had indeed got to Casey. He was stunned; knew, of course, that Corey Lomas had ambition and grabbed land any way he could, but he had never even hinted that he might have any interest in the J Bar C.

His place was almost as large as Casey's and he had plenty of water, would have even more when he built his dam, lush graze, timber for fences or houses — hell, he could build a small town with the amount of trees on their twin holdings . . .

His mind had wandered with the

thoughts racing through his brain and he suddenly became aware that the onlookers were scattering. There was a heavy though brief dragging sound almost at his feet.

Instinctively, he stepped back and saw that Tripp had taken advantage of his momentary lapse of attention and had managed to snare his sixgun which had fallen on to the boardwalk near him.

The man rolled on to his back, teeth bared, the Colt held in both hands as he thumbed back the hammer . . .

Casey fired the rifle one-handed. He couldn't possibly miss at that range. Tripp was smashed down by the lead taking him squarely through the heart and his own gun fired wild, leaping from his hand and thudding back to the worn and gritty boardwalk.

Casey looked down at the dead man at his feet and thought that at least he would have a side arm now. But the only way he was going to know if Tripp was speaking gospel or just trying to save his neck was to get on back to the J Bar C just as fast as the paint could carry him.

4

Return

He was not far north of Fort Meade when he first had the bad feeling.

He had always followed his hunches although he didn't get them very often — perhaps that was *why* he followed them when he did have them. Now, a few miles north of Sturgis and Fort Meade he got this irritating itch between his shoulder blades. It could have been some left-over nerve dancing a jig in the area of the long-healed bullet wound, but because the wound *had* healed over long ago and hadn't troubled him in any way since, Casey figured he better consider this before he dismissed it out of hand.

The country was ripe for any bushwhacker who wanted to waylay travellers, except that it was so close to the town, with Fort Meade practically at the end of Main Street, anyone figuring to pot-shot at some rider would have to be either stupid — or desperate.

He slid the rifle loose in the old saddle scabbard that had come with the Winchester.

The sixgun rig he had taken off Tripp was slung round his waist. He had done some work on the Colt — donated two hours labour to a gunsmith in exchange for a new sear and spring, the traditional weaknesses in the Frontier Model Colts, and spent some night hours working to replace these parts and tune the weapon. It shot about as good as he could expect of any sixgun, which was to say, shooting at anything over eight or ten feet was chancy. But as most gunfights were settled at these distances or less it didn't really matter.

He shouldn't have let his mind wander to such trivialities, although he was still eyeing the country he rode through without conscious thought.

But he missed the movement amongst

tumbled boulders high up a slope and didn't know a man with a rifle was hidden there until the bullet whipped air past his face.

He snatched his Winchester, dived sideways out of the saddle and hit the ground rolling. Dust enveloped him as he dropped off the low side of the trail into a ditch. Lead tore chunks of dirt and tufted grass from the broken edge.

Casey let himself slide down a little more, saw the place he wanted between two low rocks, used his legs for a rudder and clawed his way in. His legs were still a mite slow to react and a slug cut two neat holes as it passed through the loose bottoms of his buckskin breeches.

'You shoulda took a good look around that bar in Newbo, Case!'

The voice that bounced off the rocks seemed familiar but he couldn't put a name to it at first.

'Macklin?' he called, frowning, picturing the rawboned hardcase who had worked Lomas's spread as a cowhand.

'What the hell're you doin'? You never used to run with Tripp.'

'Lotta things I never *useta*, Case. You're s'posed to be dead. Figured I'd just try to put things to rights. Tripp was nothin', just someone to drift with.'

'Corey fire you?'

A mocking laugh drifted down the slope. 'You could say that. Sonuver still owes me money for helpin' rustle your herd that night. Figured if I took in your head he'd pay up — with a bonus.'

Casey was quiet, moving slowly and silently to his right, trying to get beyond the small rocks where he sprawled, hoping to catch a glimpse of Macklin's position. He saw the man just as Macklin called,

'You ain't goin' no place, Case, so don't waste time tryin' to get around me! I'm high here. I can see soon as you move an inch past them rocks where you landed.'

To back up his words, Macklin put two shots into the ground only inches from the end of the line of rocks. Casey jerked back as grit and chips of stone flew against his right side. *Damn! Macklin had him pinned, all right*.

'Corey ain't the nice feller he seems to everyone,' Macklin said, his voice hardening. 'Not even to men who've worked for him for years. Loyalty don't count with him. He uses you up and kicks your butt out . . . '

'Why don't you come on down and we'll ride in together and brace him?' Casey suggested. 'Get your own back and help me. I could likely find you a job. I've seen you work horses pretty good.'

Macklin was quiet for a short time, as if he was considering it. Then suddenly his rifle boomed and a bullet screamed off the rock in front of Casey's face. He didn't know how it missed when it ricocheted, but grit stung his eyes and made him duck real fast — and then the second bullet almost parted his hair.

As the echoes died, he heard Macklin curse.

'Last chance, Mack. Work for me or eat my lead.'

'Nah! Reckon you'd keep your word, but you couldn't pay enough and I need cash right now. Was gonna hold up the Wells Fargo office in Sturgis, but got this idea I could collect on you — '

'Sorry about this, Mack!'

Macklin laughed. 'Sorry? About *what?*'

'This!'

Casey stood abruptly, knowing this would be the last thing Macklin would expect. The rifle came up smoothly, the antler-ivory foresight sweeping over the sun-blasted high rocks, picking out Macklin in the shadow between two big boulders. He fired, three fast shots. The bullets hit the left-side boulder, instantly ricocheted into the right side, glanced off again — straight through the gap.

Only Macklin's head was in the way to prevent it ricocheting from yet another boulder. The second and third shots, hammering on the heels of the first, weren't really needed.

Macklin had barely half a face left when Casey climbed up and there wasn't a spark of life still in him. His saddle-bags yielded some food, a shirt and a part-box of cartridges. He found Macklin's horse and it was lame with a cut tendon on one foreleg, likely caused by flint from the rough country travelled through. This was probably the real reason Macklin had ambushed him: he needed a horse in good shape. Once he recognized Casey the idea of trying to collect some kind of bounty from Corey Lomas had come to him . . .

Casey reluctantly shot the lamed animal and changed the saddle for the uncomfortable Indian one on his paint. He also took Macklin's sixgun rig, saddle-bags, bedroll and hat.

After covering the dead man with rocks Casey continued riding south.

There seemed no doubt now that Corey Lomas *was* behind all the troubles that had plagued him for the last eighteen months.

God alone knew what he would find when he finally did return to his ranch in the Black Hills.

* * *

It was still a long ride but he stopped in Deadwood to see what information he could pick up.

Deadwood was still as wild as ever even though it sported a sheriff's office on the muddy main drag, but he never saw any lawman flashing his badge or gun during his time there. And there were two gunfights and one of the longest and most brutal fists-and-boots-and-all brawls he had ever seen.

Four men were taken away on doors or planks to the infirmary and it was rumoured later that one man lost an eye, another an ear, and a third one testicle and a length of bowel. Still, no law had come to break it up — or even observe the fight. A good deal of money changed hands from side bets and Casey wouldn't have minded collecting a few dollars. But to put money in his pocket he took a job at the livery, cleaning the stalls, rubbing down the horses, repairing the corral fences out back.

'Where you headed?' asked the hostler, a man named Trout, but he said everyone called him Fish. Casey could actually see the resemblance but kept it to himself.

'Going back into the Hills. Town named Keystone.'

Fish, his narrow face dark with lack of washing and beard-stubble, sniffed hard and spat on to the floor Casey had just swept clean of straw.

'Heard about the boom, huh?'

Casey must have looked puzzled, for he went on, 'Yeah, two-man-and-a-dog place for some years, couldn't give away land packages right after the War. Started to pick up a few years ago but the sodbusters got drove off by the cowmen. Heard they tried to get a railroad spur up from Rapid City but Dakota still bein' a Territory, the

Gov-mint said 'nope' and give big tracts of land to a private company — Missouri and Big Horn Express Line. Gonna run through Wyoming and swing across Montana, eventually up into Canada. 'Course, they gotta grow some, but they also gotta start somewhere.'

'And they're running a spur line out to Keystone?' Casey kept sweeping straw, trying to sound casual.

'Hell, no. They givin' that dump a miss.'

'Thought you said it was booming.'

'So 'tis. Railroad company's usin' it as a supply depot while they lay their tracks up and around a place called Yellow Hand Mountain. Say they're gonna drive a tunnel through.'

'Helluva job that'll be!'

'You know that neck of the woods?'

'Some. What makes the railroad think it'll be worth the trouble?'

'Big cattle lands openin' up in Montana. They already got a line down to Cheyenne, save a lotta trailin'. Guess they're lookin' ahead.'

Casey nodded. There was a coldness in his belly. It sounded to him like the railroad would want a lot of land, more than Congress had granted them. Was this Lomas's plan? Grab all the land he could and sell it at a premium to the — *what was it?* — Missouri and Big Horn Express Line?

The name *sounded* ambitious enough.

But then, every flim-flam he had ever heard of always started out with a flamboyant title. Not that he had any real reason for thinking this railroad company was anything but legitimate, but it was an angle that just seemed to appear in his mind — a hunch.

He spent a few days in town, asking around the bars over a couple of drinks, learned that a lot of men had headed for Keystone, on the promise of work.

'What kind?'

'Hard, mister, might-tee *hard*! Fellin' trees, grubbin' mountains flat — cain't use a lotta dynamite because the ground's unsteady or somethin' . . . '

Timber.

That was the word that kept hanging around Casey's thoughts and he heard it over and over again.

Hacking supply trails through the hills, felling logs to shore up roads for the big wagons drawn by teams of muscular oxen, bringing in lengths of track until a line could be laid so a construction locomotive could haul in the iron rails and stacks of ties . . .

Railroad ties!

By God, that was it!

Corey Lomas wasn't worried about building up a cattle ranch: he wanted the *timber* on J Bar C — the heaviest and most abundant in that part of the Black Hills, slopes crowded with oak, shagbark hickory, larch and red oak towering a hundred feet high. All woods suitable for railroad ties — and no track could be laid without them!

The man who controlled the timber for the ties was already rich. If the railroad didn't like his price, all he had to do was sit back and wait until they grew desperate enough to meet it.

He sure had underestimated Corey Lomas.

* * *

He skirted Keystone in the early dusk of a cool fall afternoon. There were some lights burning already in the town lying below in the deep shadow of the hills. On the banks of the river, he could see steam and smoke coming from a big sawmill that hadn't been there when he had left. The ring of the steel blade slicing through green timber came to him up the slope and he knew he had been right with his theory about the railroad ties. Scores of logs floated off-shore, bobbing about in this quiet part of the river, ready to be hauled into the mill.

He didn't want to run into anyone who might know him, so he rode up into the hills, smelling the piney scents and the late-flowering brush, putting his weary horse along hidden trails he had learned about when he had been searching for mavericks in the brush while opening up his own section of land.

He climbed higher than he had intended, decided now that he was up this far he might as well top-out on the crest of the ridge.

When he did, he saw scattered lights far away and below where there had been no buildings before, glowing dimly in the deepening shadow on this side of the big mountain. Someone had moved in while he had been gone. On land that had once been his.

Curious to see if whoever it was had the gall to steal his land was running cattle or felling trees, he was about to let his mount pick its way down a winding narrow trail when he heard the thud of axes.

It was full dark below, but from up here, he could see that the *other* side of the mountain, the western one, was still bathed in deep amber light, fading rapidly now. Yet the axes still bit into living timber and, listening, through the golden light he heard the swooshing crash as trees fell, tearing down younger growth, shattering branches.

They must be crazy, felling timber in the dark! Or as near as damnit to dark . . .

Crazy — or mighty greedy.

Then he heard the clash of a rifle lever behind him and felt the muzzle ram hard against his spine.

'Lift your hands as high as they'll go, then dismount. If you fall, I'll read it as an attempt to distract me while you try for your gun — and I'll shoot to kill!'

5

'Welcome Back!'

It was awkward, doing as he was ordered, but he somehow managed it without falling, although when his feet touched the ground he staggered. Out of the corner of his eye he saw the rifle barrel shift a little as if the owner had tightened the grip instinctively.

He already knew from the voice that it was a woman and now, hands still held above his shoulders, he turned slowly to face her.

'I didn't tell you to turn around!'

He kept turning until he was square-on, saw she was on foot but standing on a deadfall which explained how she was able to press the gun barrel against his spine while he was mounted.

She was raven-haired, not so shiny-dark as Sage, but it fell in natural waves to her shoulders beneath a neat-looking hat with the chinstrap pulled tight under a firm jaw. Her eyes were shadowed now but there was enough light to see they were either black or a very dark blue. Her face was narrow, but her nose was small and straight and her mouth, drawn a little tight now, maybe, was full-lipped and wide.

'Don't think I know you,' he said.

'Never mind about me. Who are you and what're you doing on my land at this time of night?'

He nodded gently: *yeah, close on dark and a strange rider obviously looking over the place*. He couldn't blame her for being suspicious and cautious.

'Name's Casey — and this used to be part of my land. Leastways, down there where the lights are.'

She was silent for a few moments, looking at him a little more closely now.

'Casey's supposed to be dead. Almost two years ago he was killed in an Indian raid on the herd he was driving to Cheyenne.'

Casey said nothing.

'I don't believe you. But I don't really care what your name is. Just get off my land and do it quick so I can see well enough to shoot you if you try anything.'

He grinned, couldn't help it. *Feisty!*

'OK. No argument there.' He turned towards his paint, ready to mount but she said,

'First you unload your sixgun and throw the bullets away.'

'Cartridges. The bullet is the lead thing at the end of the brass case . . . '

For a moment he thought she was going to pull the trigger and he stopped in mid-sentence holding his breath until it was obvious she wasn't going to shoot. Air hissed slowly between his teeth.

'Don't take me for a fool, Mister Whoever-you-are! One or two men around these parts have already discovered to their cost that that is not a wise thing to do.'

'No, ma'am — I sure won't do it again.'

'Then you may live a little longer. Now carefully, *very* carefully, unload your Colt and then just stand still.'

He worked slowly and without any fancy moves that could earn him a bullet, watching her all the time. The rifle was steady. He figured her to be in her late twenties, pushing at thirty, maybe, but she had a good form in her checked shirt and corduroy trousers tucked into the top of plain black half-boots.

'That place down there yours?' He wanted to get it right.

'Yes. It's called the Square I. Not 'eye' that you see with, but the letter 'I', first letter in my surname.'

'Which is . . .?'

'Ingram. Oh, damn you! You're trickier than I thought! Well, you might as well know the rest — I'm Margarita Ingram.'

Slight touch of an accent there . . .?

He'd thought that colouring meant

some Mexican or Spanish somewhere in the background — mother, probably, going by the surname . . .

'How'd you manage to build on my land?'

'Simple. It isn't your land and as far as I know never has been. This quarter-section was up for homesteading and my application was successful.'

'*Quarter section*! What happened to the rest? I was working a full six hundred and forty acres.'

'I know nothing about that. You'd have to see Corey Lomas. He owns most of this mountain land — *and* most of the riverbottoms.'

She watched him warily as she said it, at the same time thrusting the rifle another inch closer as he slipped his empty Colt back into his holster.

Casey smiled thinly. 'Already know that. But, I'll take your advice and go see Corey.'

She jerked her head. 'I suggest you get started. And, remember, I'll be watching you all the way down the trail.

I'm a fine shot — for a woman.'

'You're a fine woman,' he returned, settling into leather, but her face didn't change.

'What's wrong with your legs? You move — awkwardly.'

'They were busted-up for a spell. Getting better every day.' He touched a hand to the brim of Macklin's hat. '*Adios*, for now, Miss Ingram. Maybe we'll meet again.'

'It better not be on my land, Mister Whoever-you-are!'

He laughed quietly, shook his head and turned the paint, going down the western slope which was darkening slowly as the sun dipped behind the higher hills. He didn't look around but he had a bet with himself that she was doing what she had said she would — watching him all the way down.

* * *

The tree-felling had stopped now, although he could hear the axes still working as they trimmed the branches. It was a quicker, lighter sound, and he figured they were getting the logs ready for tomorrow when they would be dragged down the slope to a clear section of land above the river and then rolled in so the current could float them down to the sawmill in town.

He decided to see how many men were working the timber, if it was a permanent camp, or if they returned to the ranch bunkhouse each night. Just information that might come in handy sometime.

Casey knew this neck of the woods well enough. He dismounted and ground-hitched the paint on a patch of grass, realizing suddenly that he hadn't yet taken time to reload his sixgun. He was thumbing in the third shell when he heard a twig break under a careless boot off to his left.

He snapped the cylinder closed, thumbed the loading gate across and spun, but he was too late.

A big man stood there, covering him

with a cocked pistol and another was only a couple of yards away, also holding a gun on him.

'Leather it,' said the big man and Casey carefully put his Colt back in his holster.

'Hey, Durango!' said the second man, a rail-lean ranny Casey knew worked for Corey Lomas and whose name was Woody. 'He's wearin' Macklin's hat! An' that could be Mack's gun, too!'

Durango — Corey Lomas's hardcase bodyguard, according to Tripp. Casey didn't know him: the man must have been hired by Lomas after he had left with the trail herd.

'You run into Tripp and Macklin someplace?' Durango asked, big and solid and confident because of his size and a look in his eyes that told anyone who could read the sign, that here was a man who enjoyed watching others writhe in pain.

'Up Newbo way,' Casey replied.

'Judas, Durango!' breathed Woody,

stepping closer, 'Oh, Holy Hell! — It's *Casey*! Sonuver ain't dead at all!'

That got Durango's interest and he looked more closely at Casey. 'So. You're the famous Casey. Cat with nine lives, huh?'

'Working my way through.'

'Better watch it. They have a habit of slippin' away before you know it.' Durango stepped forward suddenly and swiped Casey across the head with his pistol.

Macklin's hat sailed half-way across the clearing and Casey dropped to his knees. Durango placed a number twelve boot against his chest and kicked him roughly to the ground. He kept the boot in the middle of the dazed man's chest, leaned forward on the bent knee, getting a little more weight into it.

'I think Mr Lomas would want to talk with you.'

Then his gun barrel cracked against Casey's head and he spun away surrounded by whirling lights and sizzling rockets.

* * *

When he came round, they had him down by the horse trough in the ranch yard, ten yards from the porch where cigarettes glowed in the darkness. The world was spinning and his eyes felt crossed and he had one *hell* of a headache as he sat up with a small, involuntary moan.

Men stirred on the porch and four of them clumped down into the yard and surrounded him. He recognized Lomas's voice as he snapped:

'Pidge, fetch a lantern.'

By the time Pidge Martell brought a storm lantern, Casey was staggering to his feet, swaying, holding his throbbing head and trying to keep the men in focus. The man who took the lantern from Pidge was Corey Lomas himself. The light showed him looking a little heavier than Casey recalled, more flabby about the jowls, the moustache a mite bushier with one or two streaks of grey.

But the eyes were the same, cold and ruthless and without mercy. The hand holding the wire handle was just as calloused and knot-knuckled.

'By hell, you were right, Woody. It damn well *is* Case! Now how in hell did you get outta that big bad river up there when the boys took your cows off you?'

'Just — lucky, I guess,' said Casey, more breathless than he liked. 'You've put on weight, Corey.'

'I eat well these days. Where the *hell* you been? The boys've been keepin' an eye out for you, just in case, but nary a sign. Where'd you hide?'

'I was a long ways north. Some Sioux found me.'

'And you've still got all your hair? Well, most. I see you lost some over your left ear.'

'That was one of the cheatin' sons of bitches you hired to hit my herd, Corey!'

Lomas laughed, looked at Durango. 'See? He's got a brain on him. Trouble is he only uses it for stayin' within the law.'

'Never had any reason to ride outside it.'

'Well, no matter. Why the hell you have to come back . . . ? No, don't bother answerin'. Know why. But you're gonna be disappointed, *amigo*. J Bar C don't exist no more. It's now all part of the Candlestick. That's what I've called this place, the brand's a big 'L' with a twist on the upright like a candle.' He turned and flung a hand towards the long log cabin and the other ranch buildings. 'How you like it? Told you I was good at buildin' cabins . . . '

Casey blinked as he looked around, barely making out the details of the ranch house.

'That the one you were gonna build me while I drove your cows to Cheyenne?'

'Believe it was. Got kinda carried away. Liked this place better than where I'd set up my own cabin and figured, what the hell? I was gonna own all this land soon as the boys took your herd away from you, anyway. So . . . here I am.'

'Thieving son of a bitch!'

Casey stumbled as he lunged forward and Lomas grinned, stepping back. Durango kicked Casey's legs from under him and he sprawled on the hard ground.

'Don't get up, Case. Durango'll only put you down again.' Corey Lomas squatted, holding the storm lantern close enough for Casey to feel the heat from the glass on his face. 'Needed money to throw up a dam, Case, a big one. Seemed an easy way to get it, killin' you, takin' your herd. Worked out well. I own all the mountain now, even had a little bit left over I had no use for — '

'Not enough timber?' cut in Casey, speech a little slurred. 'Or the wrong kind?'

Lomas lost his smirk and bantering manner. He shoved the lantern suddenly against the left side of Casey's face and the man yelled and jerked back. Lomas back-handed him casually.

'Smart! Like I said. Yeah, well it won't do you no good. I'm king o' the dungheap in these parts, me and my — pardner.'

'And who's that? The feller owns the sawmill in Keystone?'

'By hell! You blamed well *are* a smart one! Too bad we couldn't've gotten together on this deal.' Then Lomas laughed, thrust his face close to Casey's. 'But you wasn't smart enough, Case. You never seen the paper you signed that said all — *all* — your land come to me as compensation should you lose all my cattle through *any reason*, Act of God or man, before you got to Cheyenne. And, you did lose 'em!'

Casey frowned. 'I never signed anything like that!'

'Well, you signed the agreement we had that I pay you ten per cent of the sellin' price. I just left a little room on the paper and added the other afterwards. Had it witnessed, too. Legal as they come and water-tight.'

Casey had nothing to say: *he* had been the fool, not following his hunch that Lomas had some double-cross a'brewing at the time of the trail drive. Then:

'Where's Reno?' He swore at himself for almost forgetting the oldster who had stayed behind to get the new cabin started while he was on the trail drive.

Corey Lomas looked around him, stared at the ranch house. 'Aw — he's around somewheres, I guess. Haven't seen him in a while . . . '

Why did that get a laugh from the cowboys?

Casey was about to say Macklin had told him the old man had 'disappeared', but Corey suddenly stood with a sigh. 'Well, Durango — looks like Mr Casey's outlived his usefulness, so — '

'Lot of folk know I'm alive — and here, Corey,' Casey cut in. 'Fellers who saw me kill Tripp in Newbo, others in Deadwood. Stopped off in Keystone before I rode out here, too. Hell, even your neighbour over the hill stopped and passed the time of day . . . Miss Ingram, ain't it?'

Lomas frowned deeply, puckered up his mean mouth as he stared hard at Casey.

'I'll drop him off the canyon into the wildest part of the river, boss,' Durango offered and Lomas considered it but finally shook his head.

'Nah. He might be lyin', but he's savvy enough to take precautions, let someone know he's alive and was coming to see me.' Lomas kicked Casey suddenly in the ribs, doubling the man up. He stooped down. 'Case — you get off my land and you don't come back. Set one foot on it, one goddamn *toe*, and you're a dead man! Forget this place and what you had. It's all gone now, all tied up legal. You got nothin' here. Best thing for you is to ride on.' The grin widened, tight and smug. 'Durango and the boys here'll see you on your way . . . ' As he turned, he swung back. 'Oh, by the way — welcome back!'

They had already relieved him of his sixgun and knife. He was weaponless, defenceless and although he bucked and struggled as the three cowmen moved in on him, he didn't have a chance.

First it was boots — coming at him from every direction, smashing through the arms and hands he used to try to protect his face and head, stomping on his legs and belly. The commotion brought up more cowhands from the long bunkhouse connected to one end of the cabin by a covered dog-run. Side bets were quickly placed: how many bones would be broken; how long would it take for him to pass out; how many punches would he throw trying to fight back — and so on.

Through the roaring in his ears and the jarring against his body, Casey heard them and it made him mad — *Goddamn good and mad!*

With a roar that came from somewhere deep down in his battered body, he lunged up and his clawed hands sank into Woody's crotch. He squeezed and squeezed and twisted and yanked while the cowpoke yelled and screamed blue bloody murder. What was more, Casey spun Woody around, holding him close with one arm, the man taking crippling blows meant for him. Woody grew heavy and Casey made a mistake. He flung him away from him into the path of one of his attackers, found himself facing big Durango and grinned.

'How you doin' today, *amigo*?' he asked and spat a mouthful of blood into that rugged face, followed through, smashing his forehead across the bridge of the man's nose. It broke and blood gushed. Durango roared and spun away, clawing at his face.

Three or four others closed in and crowded close so Casey couldn't get a decent swing. They hammered him brutally but he refused to go down. Then they were flung aside and

Durango stood there, swaying, glassy-eyed, face masked with blood and his nose hammered on to his left cheek. One huge hand fisted up the front of Casey's buckskin shirt.

'Matter of fact — *amigo*, I'm — doin' — good!'

The last word was followed by a clubbing hammerblow from his other fist. Casey felt his legs turn to rubber but he was held up so he couldn't fall and that massive fist buried itself to the wrist in his mid-section.

After that, he lost count of how many times they hit him before he passed out.

6

Iron Man, Iron Fists

She said to him as she stood by the bunk where he lay, looking down at the ragged-edged bandages and a few strips of plaster she had had on hand, 'You don't exactly look it right now, but you're quite the iron man, aren't you?'

Casey didn't even try to grin or to move anything but his eyes in their bruised and swollen sockets: he had learned quickly that to move any muscles, even a finger or his bandaged hand, or his split lips, caused more agony than he cared for right now.

'Gimme — time,' he rasped. 'I'll — show you.'

Margarita Ingram nodded slowly. 'Yes, I saw it in you that first evening on the high trail on the mountain. I suspected then you thought you were tough and you'd come back for only one thing — to square away with Corey Lomas.'

'If I didn't — have the mind to — do — that then — I — sure do — now.'

This small room with saddle gear, bridles and as-yet-unworked tanned hides scattered around, was the first thing he saw when he came round after the beating.

He had no recollection of how he got here or even where 'here' was until the girl had showed up with a bowl of hot water and some iodine and an old sheet torn into strips for bandages.

'How . . . ?' he managed to grate as she went to work and he tried not to wince too much or gasp at the pain: *Idiot! What the hell did it matter? He felt like he'd been dragged by a horse and any man would give a twitch or two under those circumstances . . .*

She knew, too, that he was trying to tough it out, smiled slowly and said, 'I know it must hurt. Yell away all you want. I'm the only one here. My men are down in the bunkhouse.' She wrung out the cloth, poured iodine on to a piece of clean rag and then dabbed at cuts and swellings on his face. Breath hissed between his clenched teeth.

'My wrangler found you just over my line, roped to your saddle. By the way, he said that's an Indian pony you were riding.'

'Black Hills Sioux. Stayed with 'em — a — spell.'

She sobered and stared for a moment, then nodded. 'So that's where you've been these past couple of years. Lucky charm?' she asked, fingering the bullet on the cord around his neck. He explained briefly and she gave him a strange look. 'It was lucky for you, I guess. Finding friendly Indians. Everyone here thought you were dead.'

'Didn't know that — wouldn't've cared — if I — had.'

'Well, I'm sure it came as a surprise to Corey Lomas to find out you're still alive.'

Casey grunted. 'Had Durango beat

up on me to welcome me back.'

'An awful man, Durango. Arrogant bully, actually enjoys inflicting pain. He drove off some of the riverbottom farmers for Lomas simply by beating them up so badly, or burning their houses, that the rest just packed up and moved out before they received the same kind of treatment.'

'What was — Dodge doing?'

'Sheriff Dodge? He was here before you left, then? I believe he wants a law-abiding County but his hands are fairly well tied. You see, Lomas's partner in the sawmill is Judge Bligh. And any — transgressions of the law by Lomas are soon rearranged to make them legal, or borderline legal. Sheriff Dodge is a very frustrated man and — well, I think he's slowly giving up, just content now to sit back and let things flow wherever Lomas and the judge want them to. He's given up fighting them and considers himself lucky still to have a job, especially one that pays so well.'

'How come?'

'Keystone is a boom town now. That means prices of everything are booming. It's said that for every drunk Dodge gets off the street, he's paid five dollars by the business folk. Which means a night's work can be equivalent to almost a month's wages . . . '

'Never figured — Waylon Dodge — like that.'

'He's a married man now. Has a year-old son. Family men are usually — circumspect.'

He grunted, let her finish patching him up.

'How come you're doing this? You were gonna shoot me before.'

She hesitated, rolled down her shirt sleeves, looked at him steadily. 'I didn't believe you were who you said. I'd heard a little about Casey, the man who originally set out to homestead most of this mountain, then drove a herd of cattle towards Cheyenne and was killed in an Indian raid. No one has mentioned you for a long time, I'm afraid.'

He smiled ruefully. 'That won't keep me awake nights.'

She gave him a half-smile back. 'No, I don't expect it will — but my wrangler recognized you. A man named Mustang Givens, who most folk call Musty. Said he was working these hills when you were here before.'

'Uh-huh. Good man with horses. We did some business.'

'Yes. He says you're honest and no friend of Lomas. That was what decided me to — well . . . ' She shrugged.

'Mighty grateful, ma'am — I'll be outta here soon's I can get on my feet.'

She pushed firmly against his shoulders as he tried to sit up and swing his legs over the side of the low bunk.

'You stay put. And I mean for at least three to five days.'

'The hell with that! If you'll pardon the French.'

She was already at the door, turning slightly to look at him over her shoulder. 'Five days would be best.'

'Listen, I . . .'

The door closed on his words and he sank back, surprised he was so much out of breath after the slight exertion. After a while he nodded to himself.

Damn, but he was sick and tired of lying-up in bed, having womenfolk take care of him! First Sage, now this one.

OK! Five days. A week. As long as it took for him to recover . . . or until the woman kicked him off her spread. What the hell had she called it . . . ? Square I. Queer name — but it would be his home until he could get around, sit a saddle — and shoot a gun again.

Then, Corey Lomas, old feller, you just better watch out.

Aloud he said, staring up at the ceiling, 'You, too, Durango — and Woody and Pidge and Long Frank and Baldy Reems. *All of you — Watch out!* Because Casey is coming and there'll be a gun in his hand.'

* * *

He was four days before he could walk around the small ranch yard unassisted and he swore softly to himself every minute he was delayed from riding the paint. The wrangler, Mustang Givens — Musty — had taken care of the animal and Casey sought him out at the bunkhouse. They shook hands as Casey thanked him for bringing him in and taking care of the paint.

He was a short man, wiry, in his late forties and feeling the effects of long years of gut-busting, bone-breaking rough riding. Long hair hung to his shoulders and he always seemed to be wearing at least three days' beard growth. But he was a grinner: every time he spoke he grinned, showing chipped and gapped teeth.

'You still look like hell, but way better than when I found you. That paint's a good hoss. Was gonna put shoes on him but figured you might like to decide that.'

'Yeah, aimed to get around to it.'

'I'll take care of it before you leave. If you do.'

'I'll leave here, but I'll stick around the hills. Lomas done me wrong, Musty, but what I can't figure is Dodge sitting the fence.'

'Easy enough — he married Judge Bligh's niece.'

'So that's it — Bligh on one side, wife on the other telling him to leave her uncle be. Listen, what happened to Reno, Musty? Lomas reckons he's still around someplace.'

Musty scratched at his beard. 'Well, he might be. He sure was riled when Lomas started takin' over buildin' that cabin, s'posed to be for you. Told me once over a beer in the saloon in town that he had a mind to ride back into the hills and join Butch Satterlee and friends.'

'Who the hell's Butch Satterlee?'

'Homesteader from the riverbottoms. Tough *hombre*, but not as tough as he thinks. Lomas and Durango kicked him off but Butch stayed up in the hills. Kills himself a Lomas steer once in a while, hauls down fences, lets cows run free, generally causes a bit of hell every now and again.'

Casey frowned. 'Might keep him in mind. But Reno's a mite too old for that kind of thing.'

'You heard him cuss-out Lomas you wouldn't think so. Never seen him so riled. But I dunno where he is — Satterlee is just a guess.'

* * *

By the end of the week, Casey was sitting the paint, newly shod by Mustang. It took him a couple more days to ride further than the Square 'I' boundary and pushing the animal up the heavily timbered slopes he found to be exhausting.

'Not as spry as you thought,' Margarita Ingram commented at supper that night, giving him a half-smile.

'Getting there,' he replied shortly. Then, after a short silence, he said, 'Figure to ride up the draw tomorrow and start shooting. Will it bother your cows up that way?'

She shook her head, the raven hair glinting in the lamplight and he had a flash of Sage bending over the campfire as she cooked venison and fish.

Margarita looked very anxious as she looked across at Casey now. 'You're going to start a shooting war?'

'Could come to that. I don't aim to be caught by Durango or Lomas's men again. Someone'll die before they get their hands on me a second time.'

She nodded as she ate but didn't speak until she had cleared her plate. She drank some coffee.

'You're preparing for an all-out range war.'

'Thought Lomas had already started it . . . and Butch Satterlee was keeping it going.'

'Well, Lomas did start things, riding roughshod over the settlers. Butch, I'm not sure about. He *wants* to stand up to Lomas but he's sort of half-hearted. Still, he is harassing Corey, which is the main thing, I suppose.'

'That why you leave out supplies for him?'

Her cup rattled against her saucer. 'How did you . . .?'

'Rode up as far as Boney Ridge.' It was a place used by the Indians long ago to stampede buffalo over a cliff and then kill the survivors before butchering and skinning. Bleached bones were still piled thirty feet high at the base. 'Found a box sticking out from under a bush. The ground got washed away in that heavy rain we had couple nights back. You left a note, told Butch I'd come back, might be joining him.'

She sighed. 'I thought you might be able to help each other. You're a stubborn man, Casey, especially when you're wronged, I suspect. Yes, I leave a few supplies for Butch and his friends now and again. He had a rough deal. I think he knows he can't win against Lomas, but he still stays on!'

Casey smiled. 'Lomas give you a hard time?'

'No-o, not really. He doesn't like me

being here and I don't like his methods. Lucky for me, he's not interested in this side of the mountain.'

'For now.'

She arched her dark eyebrows. 'You think I'll have trouble with him sometime?'

'You'd be foolish not to be ready for it. He's a landgrabber. I got along OK with Corey, but I never did trust him. That's why I insisted we have a contract for him paying me ten per cent of the selling price of his cows. Biggest mistake I ever made, it seems. My own fault, but I'll put it right.'

'Just like that.'

'It won't be easy. But I haven't got the full picture yet. I'll see what Dodge and the judge have to say.'

She jumped. 'You — you're not going to — brace them, are you? Bligh runs the whole county, not just the town, and Sheriff Dodge can't do anything about it.'

'Maybe he just thinks he can't — maybe he only needs someone to show him how he can have a say in things.'

As she cleared the dishes, she said quietly, 'I think you're biting off more than you can chew, Casey. It would probably be better if you simply accepted your luck — good and bad — and rode on.'

'You don't really believe that,' he said flatly. She rattled the dishes in the clay sink, using the noise so she could avoid answering.

Casey smiled thinly: she didn't fool him. She *wanted* him to go after Lomas, all out . . .

⋆ ⋆ ⋆

Sheriff Waylon Dodge glanced up from reading a copy of the *Deadwood News* and frowned, shoulders stiffening a little as he recognized the tall man in buckskins entering his office. He set down the paper and watched Casey approach, then stood, offering his right hand. They gripped and Dodge motioned to a chair piled high with old newspapers.

'Tip 'em off and set you down, Case.'

Casey did so, took the tobacco sack and papers the lawman offered. Both men got their smokes going before either spoke again. Dodge was about Casey's age but looked older than Casey remembered.

'Heard you'd come back from the dead.'

'The *almost* dead, Waylon. Seems you got yourself married while I been away.' The sheriff seemed to tense a little but nodded. 'To Judge Bligh's niece.'

Dodge's eyes narrowed. 'Fine woman, Lucille. Loves her uncle. Gave me a great little son.'

'Good to hear it. Tie your hands some? Family, I mean.'

Dodge leaned back in his chair, looking Casey over carefully. 'You hear that someplace?'

'Must've, I guess. True?'

Waylon Dodge took his time answering. 'It's — awkward. Lucille likes

— nice things. The boy's a great little tyke but he keeps poorly, needs a deal of medical attention. The judge helps out . . . '

'And the business folk pay five bucks for every drunk you get off the streets.'

'OK. It's easy money. The judge sort of — arranges things to suit himself. Don't leave a lot for me to do.'

'How about out of town? In the hills?'

'If you mean that Butch Satterlee, I'll catch up with him sooner or later . . . '

'You know who I mean, Waylon.'

Dodge's gaze was steady and cold. 'Corey Lomas. I've had a lot of complaints, but when I check 'em out and bring in the evidence to the judge he never finds anything illegal on Corey's part. I'm in no position to say different.'

'If you *think* there's something illegal, you can speak up.'

'I run things the best way I can, Casey.'

Casey stood slowly. 'No, you don't.

And you know it.'

Dodge stood, too, tapping fingers against his desk edge. 'What I do know is I'm still sheriff around here and in that capacity, I'm warnin' you not to start any trouble.'

'I'll remember, Waylon. Was gonna say 'nice seeing you again', but — don't think I'll bother.'

Casey made for the door. Dodge's mouth tightened.

'You watch yourself, Casey!'

As he went out, Casey wondered if that was a warning to be careful — or not to kick over the traces . . .

* * *

He was going to see Judge Bligh but went into the Tall Trees saloon instead. The streets were crowded with heavy supply wagons and he figured they must be picking up on behalf of the railroad. Tough-looking men in mud-spattered clothes walked a mite arrogantly along the boardwalks. The stores seemed to have a lot more goods displayed in their windows than when he had last been here. Prices were mighty high, too.

The ringing of the steam-driven saws in the mill down on the sloping riverbank penetrated everywhere in town. The wood-fired donkey-engines thumped and thudded. There was none of the old peace he remembered in Keystone now. Even the river was different, crowded with logs, jammed in one or two places with men working with long pry bars to free them, jumping expertly from log to log. Looked like there were a lot of experienced lumberjacks in town.

And there were plenty in the crowded bar of the Tall Trees. He shouldered his way through and got jammed by a couple of men arguing. As he stepped around them, he glanced in the dirty bar mirror — and went very still.

Reflected in the fly-specked and smeared glass he saw a couple of familiar faces. Long Frank Donahue and Baldy Reems, two of the men who had beaten him out at Lomas's ranch. Suddenly he shoved the two arguing lumberjacks to one side, strode up behind Lomas's men and jammed his body in between them as they hunched over their drinks. Startled, Long Frank and Baldy began to straighten and turn — but not fast enough.

Casey grabbed each by the back of the neck and slammed them face first into the zinc edge of the counter. Men scattered as the hardcases groaned and fell to their knees, faces bloody, eyes dazed. Baldy Reems looked at the clots of blood dripping into his hand and glanced up, not recognizing Casey yet through his blurred vision.

'You bust my nose!'

'And I'm about to bust your ribs!' Casey gritted, driving a boot into the man's side. Mustang Givens had sold him a pair of proper riding-boots and now they bent Baldy's ribs so that the man moaned and fell on to his side, writhing.

Long Frank could see who his

attacker was now and he started up, groggy, bloody but game, reaching for his gun. He froze when Casey's Colt appearcd in his hand, cocked, rock-steady, braced against his hip. His eyes widened and he shot his hands high, shaking his head.

Casey stepped forward and gun-whipped him brutally to the floor, a back-and-forth motion with the gun barrel. Long Frank lay very still, hat askew, knees drawn into his belly.

There was a cleared circle around Casey now and the barkeep stared, squinting.

'Hell, that you, Casey? Goddamnit, man, the hell you doin' in my bar?'

'Give me a red-eye and a beer chaser, Milt,' Casey said as he holstered his gun, kicked the moaning Baldy aside and braced the counter. He looked around at the staring customers. 'What a man has to do to get himself a drink, eh?'

That got a laugh and the barkeep slapped the drinks on the counter top.

'Have 'em on the house. Then go and don't come back.'

'You always did favour Corey Lomas, as I recollect, Milt. But thanks for the drinks.'

He downed them both, turned to leave and found Sheriff Waylon Dodge standing inside the batwings, a shotgun held in both hands.

'Let's go see the judge, Case.'

7

Judge and Jury

He hadn't seen such a change in any man, except for a couple who survived the torture post of the Comanche on the *Llano Estacado* one time, as he saw in Judge Lawrence Bligh.

The man had put on a massive amount of weight. Casey recalled him as a moderately heavy man but one who held himself well and dressed in clothes that helped give him a look that was attractive to the ladies.

Now his big belly bulged and prevented him from pulling his swivel chair any closer to the massive desk cluttered with papers. The bottom four buttons on his vest were undone, allowing a small triangle of hairy white flesh to show through the straining shirt which seemed to have popped a button or two. There was cigar ash spilled down the same vest and his collar was undone, the string tie pulled down. His face was flabby, red and sweaty, his hair abundant but somehow looked unhealthily colourless. His eyes were sunken back in deep sockets, smudged grey underneath.

He glared now at Casey and flicked his eyes to Waylon Dodge who still held the shotgun, but uncocked and down at his side.

'Just walked in and mashed 'em against the bar, that right?' wheezed Bligh.

The sheriff nodded. 'Wasn't but five minutes since I'd warned him in my office not to start trouble, Judge.'

'Well, what I remember of Casey he was always a troublemaker, went hunting it, on the prod.'

'You're thinking of someone else, Judge,' Casey said.

'Shut your mouth, till I tell you to open it!' Bligh slammed a fat-fingered hand down on to the desk, scattering some papers and glaring.

'Those two men had beat the crap outta me,' Casey said defiantly. 'How the hell you think I got to look like this?'

The judge's eyes almost disappeared into the folds of flesh around them, and his breath wheezed. He tapped his big fingers on the desk top — one, two, three, four, five; one, two, three, four, five . . .

'Thought I told you to be quiet,' he said very softly. 'I'm used to being obeyed in my court, mister.'

Casey looked around at the untidy, badly furnished office. 'Didn't realize this was a court room, Judge.'

'My court room's wherever I say it is!'

Casey felt the chill creeping up from his belly into his chest. He glanced at Dodge who was standing there looking uncomfortable and avoiding Casey's eyes.

'This isn't a trial, judge,' Casey said quietly.

Bligh surprised him by smiling coldly, fat lips stretching out but not revealing his teeth. 'It's whatever I say it is, Casey. You don't seem to savvy the position you're in.'

'I knocked out two fellers who'd kicked and beat me while I was either being held or lying on the ground. Don't seem to me to be any case to answer. Stretch it a mite and you could get disturbing the peace, maybe, but — '

'How about assault and battery on two gents just minding their own business, having a quiet drink?' Judge Bligh suggested.

'I just told you what they'd done to me — '

'What you *allege* they done to you. I don't see any witnesses on your behalf. Would you like time to try and find some?'

The smirk was still there on that fat face. He knew Casey couldn't produce any witnesses.

'Happened at Lomas's spread, Judge. Long Frank and Baldy work for him — '

'So, what you were really doing was getting back at Corey Lomas indirectly by attacking his men. Because he's built that trash place you left into something worthwhile, I suppose.' Bligh shook his massive head. 'Nothing worse than a sorehead can't make it, then resents someone comes along and does a hell of a good job on the mess he left . . . ' He flicked his gaze to Dodge. 'You look like you're busting to say something, Waylon.'

'I — figured maybe disturbing the peace, Judge. Give him a few days in the cell block, maybe a little time workin' in your mill. Then kick him outta town.'

Bligh shook his head, side to side, slowly. 'Ah, you — you're way too soft, Waylon. Lucille has told me so on several occasions. 'Uncle,' she says, 'Waylon is just an old softy deep down. Y'ought to see him play with little Larry — It's a sheer delight.'' He nodded now, pursing fat lips. 'Mighty nice to know that great-nephew of mine has your love and affection, Waylon, but you got to show a sterner side if you want to be a good sheriff. You leave this to me. This son of a bitch has come back for only one thing — to make trouble for Corey Lomas. And he does that, he makes trouble for me, seeing as Corey's my partner in the sawmill and one or two other ventures . . .'

'How're your shares in the Missouri and Big Horn Express, Judge?' Casey asked and knew it was a mistake. *That* just about put the cap on whatever Bligh had in mind for him.

'So, we have us a real smart-mouth here, do we? Waylon, I want you to lock this man up in your cell block, give him a cell to himself, I don't want him corrupting any other inmates you might have or take in. I'll arrange for him to be transferred to Fort Wingate Territorial Prison soon as can be fixed.'

He winked at Casey who had gone very still, perhaps paled a little at the judge's words. Fort Wingate Prison was in the north-east of Dakota, just short of the Canadian border, and colder than a polar bear's ass, according to rumour. It was reserved for the Territory's really bad *hombres* and none ever left there unless they had served their sentence or died. Breakouts had been tried but not for a *very* long time — even in summer it was a corner of hell up that way.

Dodge cleared his throat. 'Judge — I — I dunno if you can do that.'

Bligh wheezed like the safety valve on one of the donkey-engines in his sawmill as he swung around in his chair. 'Who you talking to, boy?'

'Judge, I mean, even assault and battery is only a couple of months in the local hoosegow . . . '

'Exactly right, Waylon. You ain't as dumb as you look, are you? Couldn't be, I guess. Look, it's time to show scum like this Casey that they can't come into my town and take the law into their own hands.' He raised a fat hand as Dodge started to protest. 'I'm not criticizing your work, boy, though I could without much effort. What I'm saying, I aim to make an example of Casey here and it's just his bad luck that he's come before me when I've decided to crack down on men like him.'

'The fact that it'll get me out of the way, give you and Lomas a free run, don't enter into it, does it, Judge?'

Bligh sighed and Dodge hissed sharply, 'Shut up, Case!'

'You just dug yourself a hole you'll never find a way out of, you stupid son of a bitch!' Bligh told Casey. 'Waylon, get the manacles on him and throw him in your cells. I've got some paperwork to do so's I can get him into the system right away. Now, don't you be scared of him! You're acting according to my directions and I'm the law around these parts . . . ' He looked steadily at Casey once more. 'And don't you forget it, mister!'

* * *

As he locked the cell door and asked Casey to put his hands through the bars so he could unshackle them, Waylon Dodge said, 'Hell, I'm sorry about this, Case. Never figured it'd get so out of hand.'

'Well, I'm glad you spoke up and did all you could for me, Waylon.'

Dodge stiffened at the sarcasm in Casey's voice, wrenched off the manacles and stepped back, jaw jutting.

'You — don't understand! I — I've got Lucille and little Larry to think of . . .'

'Sure — set the kid the best example you can and hope he grows up just like you.' Casey curled a lip and turned away, dropping on to the bunk and locking his hands behind his head, staring up at the dirty ceiling.

He didn't hear the sheriff leave.

* * *

Lucille Dodge was a fine-looking woman, red-haired, ivory-skinned, in her mid-twenties, and pretty happy with her lot. Her baby boy was wonderful, prone to catching all kinds of colds and tummy upsets, but Uncle Lawrence saw to it that he had the best doctors, even sending her and the child down to Denver one time. Her husband was the town sheriff and had a good future ahead of him — or so the Judge assured her and she wouldn't argue with *him*.

'I ran into Uncle earlier, outside Ridgway's store, Waylon,' she told him over their meal. 'He's very pleased with you. Said you acted real fast earlier today and caught a troublemaker almost red-handed. 'That's the kind of lawman we want in this town,' he said. Oh, I'm so pleased for you Waylon! I told you that Uncle Lawrence would take care of you.'

'Yeah — he was happy I caught this particular feller,' Dodge murmured, to be sociable. The baby was sleeping in another room. He suddenly stood. 'Lucille, I've got to ride out of town for a spell. May be late for supper. Just keep it in the oven or make something cold and I'll have it when I get in.'

She looked at him sharply. 'Where're you going?'

'Have to check some papers with that Ingram woman — should've done it a couple days ago.' She still didn't look convinced and he smiled, leaned down and kissed her lightly on the cheek. 'Don't want Uncle to think I'm neglecting the small details of my job, do we . . .?'

'Oh — I see. Yes, well, try not to be too late.'

'I won't. I have to relieve Ed Clyde later. He can't do his full shift tonight.'

'Waylon, you must be more assertive! You're his boss. He's only a deputy. You *tell* him he has to do his full night shift.'

'Normally I would, but I did say he could have this time off a while back — and I've got that Casey feller in the cells. Want to make sure he's safe there.' He widened his grin as he set his hat on his head. 'Uncle said he wants me to keep a close eye on him.'

That satisfied her and not long after he rode out of town and took the winding trail up into the hills that led to

Margarita Ingram's ranch. As soon as he was away from town, he raked the spurs into his mount's flanks and lashed with the rein ends, urging the startled horse to more speed.

He didn't have a lot of time to spare.

* * *

Ed Clyde was just swinging his boots up on to the spare straightback, lounging in the sheriff's own swivel-chair, preparing for a quiet night in the law office, when Waylon Dodge appeared in the street doorway.

Startled, Clyde let his boots fall with a thud to the floor and struggled to get out of the swivel-chair. Dodge stepped inside, lifting a hand.

'Relax, Ed. I'll take my chair if you don't mind, though. I'm beat.'

The deputy, young and fit and something of a ladies' man, ran a hand a mite nervously over his slicked-back hair and dusted off both chairs with a spotted bandanna as Dodge slumped into the swivel-chair. He was dusty and sweaty and he yawned.

'Look like you been ridin' hard, Waylon.'

'Had an out-of-town chore to do — Lucille and the boy're asleep. I'm all keyed-up from ridin'. Won't be able to sleep. You want to slip away and see that ginger-haired waitress works tables at the Regal — you go ahead, Clyde. You ought to just about catch 'em closin' if you go straight away.'

Clyde's jaw hung open a little and he blinked, trying to absorb the sheriff's offer. *First Dodge says he's beat, then he's too wide awake to sleep . . .*

Dodge waved tiredly. 'Go on. Go an' see your lady. I've got plenty work here I can do or I might end up dozin' in my chair. It's OK. Only Casey in the cells and it's quiet tonight on the streets.' He smiled and winked. 'Happen to know it's Ginger's birthday so I hope you've bought her a bunch of flowers or somethin'. Go have yourself a good time.'

This sure wasn't like Waylon Dodge, but . . .

'Well, thanks, Waylon! *Thanks!* Gee, when I asked before for tonight off you said — '

Dodge looked at him sharply. 'Ed — it's what I'm sayin now that counts. Get along with you. And wish Ginger a happy birthday from me.'

'I surely will, Waylon! Surely will. Thanks again!'

The deputy snatched his hat and ran out into the night. The streets were fairly quiet, but that was to be expected: payday at the sawmill wasn't until week's end and the men were mostly broke. The few who had money didn't have enough to throw a real wingding, or couldn't afford enough booze to put them on the prod, looking for trouble.

Dodge sighed, tossed his hat at a wall peg and missed. He rolled and smoked a cigarette, glanced at the big, slow-pendulum cottage-clock on the wall above the gun cupboard. *Ten-thirty*.

He dozed a little, kept waking himself up to look at the clock. When it showed eleven o'clock, he stood, walked through the darkened cell block, hearing Casey's snoring, and went to the rear door. He checked the lock, jiggling the key. The sound must have wakened Casey for as Dodge went back past his cell, the man asked,

'It supper time yet?'

Dodge didn't answer but swore softly under his breath. He had forgotten to tell someone at the diner down the street to bring a meal in for his prisoner. Ah, well, Casey could stand it for a little longer . . .

In the front office, Dodge opened the street door a little after first blowing out the lamp. It was quieter than ever out there now, hardly anyone on the street and no one in this vicinity. He slipped out into the night, pulling the door to behind him, going through the motions of locking it, adjusted his hat and then started out for home.

His heart was hammering against his ribs as he hurried down the street.

* * *

Casey was annoyed that he hadn't been given any supper and also riled at the sheriff for rattling the damn lock on the rear door so loudly. The man ought to be able to lock up his cell block a lot more quietly than that. You'd think he did it deliberately to disturb his sleep.

He tried to settle again but felt wide awake now and, easing on to his left side, was pulling up the worn blanket when he froze, snapping his gaze into the darkness.

Someone was rattling the damn lock on the rear door again! What the hell . . .

He swung his legs slowly off the bunk, frowning.

The door was opening . . .

Then he heard low voices and two men crowded inside. He glimpsed a third man's head and shoulders briefly silhouetted against the stars.

The hell was going on!

The two men groped into the passage and he heard one at the unlit lantern dangling on a wall peg by its wire handle. A match scraped and flared and outlined the man holding the lantern as he touched the flame to the wick, set the glass chimney. When he swung around the light gleamed off the sixgun in his hand and the battered barrels of a sawn-off shotgun held by his companion.

'Cover him while I go get the keys from Dodge's desk,' said the man with the light. He set it down on the floor and hurried away towards the front office.

'What's going on?' Casey asked, standing at the bars now, unable to see anything much above waist-level of the man with the shotgun because the lamp was resting on the floor.

'Shut up!' the man growled, clearly edgy. 'Just do like you're told and you might live to see the sun rise.'

'*Might*?' exclaimed Casey but the man didn't answer, only poked the gun barrels between the bars and jabbed him roughly in the midriff.

'Get away from the bars or I'll break your fingers!'

Casey grunted and stepped back,

rubbing himself, mighty leery now as he heard the other one coming back from the front office jingling the keys.

What were they going to do? Drag him outside and shoot him in the back? Say he was killed while trying to escape?

That would be just the kind of thing Judge Bligh and Corey Lomas would arrange.

But it was too late now to do anything about it.

The key turned in the lock and the cell door clanged back against the bars. The man with the sixgun lunged in, grabbed him roughly and flung him out into the passage so hard he slammed into the wall opposite the cell and fell to one knee.

Brutal fingers twisted in his collar and yanked him upright, sent him staggering towards the open rear door where the third man waited.

'Move, goddamnit! Or I'll put a bullet in you right here and now!'

8

Head for the Hills

Casey had no idea where he was except that they seemed to be climbing. He smelled the scents of the different trees, so figured it had to be somewhere in the hills. Which part, he had no idea.

They had grabbed his arms and pulled them behind him when they had left the law-office yard. He saw some horses tethered in trees on the far side of the narrow stream that ran behind the sheriff's office and then they whipped a blindfold over his head and tied it so tight he thought his eyes were going to pop out of their sockets.

'Too tight!' he gritted but it only earned him another jab with the shotgun barrels. Then his arms were pulled around to the front and a rope was swiftly tied about his wrists.

'Just shut up, concentrate on stayin' in the saddle.' He recognized the voice as that of the man with the sixgun. 'You fall off and we push you over the nearest cliff — which won't be far away.'

Seemed someone chuckled at that.

They set off, downstream at first, left it and went up the bank, then his horse was jabbed in the rump with something that brought a small whinny of surprise from it before it instinctively jumped forward. Back into the stream, jarring him.

They went back upstream — he could tell by the sounds of the flowing water and the way the horse was walking — and it was a long time before they turned towards the bank.

'Duck,' someone said and he leaned forward over his mount's head, felt branches and leaves dragging across his back. They had gone ashore somewhere under a bunch of willows. He heard one rider drop back, no doubt to wipe out their tracks. The manoeuvre might fool a posse for quite a while: they would tend to follow the stream as far as the first set of tracks, still clearly showing downstream, and start searching in that direction.

But anyone with a bit of sense would figure a fugitive would head for the hills. Where, Casey figured, he would have an 'accident', no doubt fatal . . .

They must be going to set it up to make it look as if he had successfully escaped jail but come to grief during his try for freedom. A long way from town.

He wondered why. And why it took *three* of them. Those two who had come into the cellblock had been efficient enough to easily handle a job like this.

It was all too queer for him to unravel. Anyway, his head still throbbed from where it had hit the passage wall when the one with the sixgun had thrown him out of the cell.

They kept climbing and he felt the air grow cooler and knew they were going high. Then they topped-out on a sharp ridge — *Sawbuck*? — and he tipped forward in the saddle as they started down. Later, they angled across the face of the slope in a shallower ride so that he had to lean to one side, uphill, in case he fell.

They had lost him. Without the blindfold, even in the dark, he likely would be able to locate where they were, but they had him bamboozled right now — which, he guessed, was their idea.

With little notion of the time he couldn't even figure distance covered, but suddenly there were different odours; flowers, sage, sassafrass, maybe, and some berries rattled off branches as his mount scraped through a clump of brush. They were well down now, clear down to the draws and canyons in the lower foothills.

The horse began walking more slowly, placing its feet carefully, rocks clattering. *Dry creekbed*. His shoulder banged against an earthen wall and dirt crumbled, some going in the top of his riding boot. *Draw. Narrow.*

Then he felt more space about him and they stopped. Someone gave him a shove and he tumbled out of the saddle on to cushioning grass, his horse snorting and moving away. Casey struggled to his knees and he felt a knife slice through the ropes. With numbed fingers he reached up immediately and tore off the blindfold. His vision was blurred and he saw multi-images because the blindfold had been pressing against his eyeballs. But he saw enough: he was in a camp on a grassy bench, two lean-tos with sides of shaggy-oak bark and scattered bedrolls, a camp-fire's ashes, and the box, or one similar, that he had found half-hidden under a bush with supplies in it and a note from Margarita Ingram. Blinking, eyes filling with cleansing tears, he wiped a hand across his face and turned to look at his captors.

Two raggedly dressed men, one with a shotgun — he was the shorter of the two but still beefy — and —

'So the third man ain't a man at all!' he exclaimed as Margarita Ingram stepped forward and held out his sixgun rig and the Winchester '66.

'Sorry to be so dramatic but there was no time for explanations at the jail,' she said. 'Waylon had to get back and make it look good; 'discover' your escape.'

He frowned. 'Dodge was in on it?'

'He arranged it. After he put you in jail on the judge's orders, he rode out to see me, knew I was in touch with Butch.' She nodded to the big man, shag-haired and mean-faced. 'He left the rear door unlocked and gave his deputy the night off.'

'I thought all that rattling with the door was him locking things down for the night. So Waylon's got a conscience after all.'

'I didn't ask him his motives, but I believe he's a decent man, just being — crowded, by his wife and Judge Blight. Come and meet Butch Satterlee and Cotton Rix.'

Both men ignored his proferred hand and the girl frowned but Casey smiled crookedly, saying,

'Not welcome, I take it, gents.'

'Miz Ingram asked it as a favour and we owe her,' growled Butch, voice gravelly and deep. 'We do all right without any help.'

'Butch!' the girl said sharply but she knew she was not in this conversation — or was it a confrontation . . . ?

'From what I hear, you ain't done much to Lomas so far.'

The shotgun came up in Rix's hands. 'We got plans — and they don't include you.'

'OK by me — I got plans of my own.'

The girl stepped between them, glaring from one to the other. 'For heaven's sake! You all have the same objective — getting back at Lomas. Surely working together will be more productive than going at it singly!'

'Me and Cotton work well together,' Satterlee told her, sounding a mite uncomfortable. Casey would guess that he was very aware of how much he owed the ranch-woman, keeping him supplied with food and maybe ammunition. Certainly she would keep him posted on happenings in and around Keystone: vital information for men on the dodge.

'Casey knows these hills probably a lot better than you two. He's had his land stolen from him, his cattle, lost good friends to Lomas and his hardcases. You've been toying with Corey Lomas, Butch, and you know it. You have to face up to the fact that you aren't very good at planning.'

Butch bristled. 'Good enough to figure if we set fire to the timber Lomas and Bligh're outta business!'

Casey laughed shortly, the shotgun seeking him. He casually brought the Winchester around to point in Rix's direction and the man's moon face showed he didn't like it.

'Where've you two been the last few days? It's been raining, not just here, but way back in the hills. Wet timber doesn't make a good fire.'

'There's lotsa pines, trees bustin' with resin!' snapped Butch. 'They'd set off the rest no matter how wet.'

'But slowly, Butch, slow enough for a good fighting team to get the fire out before it got out of hand. And Lomas is working experienced lumberjacks. They'd have your fire out before you got off the mountain.'

Satterlee spat. 'We're gonna try, anyways. Wait till it dries if we have to.'

'Then you'll set the whole of the Black Hills ablaze and wipe out Keystone, maybe even Rapid City as well. I wouldn't like to be in the boots of the men who did that. They'd be hunted down and lynched — or tossed into the rapids and get bounced off a hundred rocks and snags. Wouldn't even recognize them as men after that.'

The men looked at each other, uneasy.

'You'd destroy a lot of ranches, put innocent people in danger, Butch,' the woman said persuasively. 'You'd be no better than Lomas.'

'Aaaahh. We'll think on it some more,' Satterlee said finally. 'You want shelter you'll have to build your own, Casey.'

'Uh-huh. But first . . .'

Casey stepped forward with one lunging move and swung the rifle barrel hard against the side of Cotton Rix's head. The man's feet left the ground and his grunt of pain and surprise covered Margarita's gasp. Butch moved in but Casey drove backwards with the rifle and the butt took the man in his big belly. He dropped to his knees, gagging.

'*What're you doing?*'

Casey shrugged, levering a shell into the rifle's breech to be on the safe side. 'They let me think they were taking me out to kill me — I just want 'em to see it won't be easy, should they really get such a notion.'

'Don't spoil it for me, Casey,' she said quietly and he frowned, not sure what she meant.

He thought she almost smiled. Then she mounted her sorrel and she said to him quietly as the outlaws slowly recovered, 'I think you might have their attention — if not a smidgen of respect. But you'll have to go easy, Casey. These are hard, bitter men and they've scores to settle. Be careful they don't see you as one of them. I must get back.'

'Obliged to you again, ma'am. Will Dodge get up a posse?'

'He'll have to to make it look good to the judge and Lomas. But he'll try to keep them away from this area.'

She wheeled the mount and rode away across the grassy bench. By then Butch and Rix were on their feet but made no move towards Casey, who faced them, rifle down at his side, thumb on the hammer spur.

'That it?' he asked. 'Or you want to try again?'

'You'll — keep!' growled Rix, grimacing.

Satterlee shrugged. 'Margarita thinks

you're a hot-shot. You'll have to show *us*.'

'Fair enough. How about some grub? And then we'll figure something out.'

'You cook your own grub.'

Casey nodded, looked at the men steadily. 'Before I do, tell me about Reno.'

They stared back at him blankly.

'Reno. Old feller I left behind to build my cabin. Someone said when Lomas moved in he came looking for you two.'

Butch and Rix both shook their heads.

'He never showed,' Satterlee said quietly, glanced at Cotton and added, 'When Lomas was building that big place of his we — we wondered why he had men diggin' a hole in the middle of the cabin space — before the floor was laid. Figured it must be for drainage of some sort.'

A cold feeling in his belly, Casey asked, 'What kind of a hole?'

Satterlee hesitated, but Rix said, 'Looked like a grave.'

* * *

If Waylon Dodge felt nervous he didn't let it show whcn Judge Bligh called him to his office. It was still early morning and there were half a dozen men gathering outside the law office across the street and down the block aways.

'How'd it happen, Waylon?' the judge asked in a level tone, his eyes deep in the bags of flesh, big fingers running up and down on the edge of his desk as he watched the sheriff.

Dodge spread his hands. 'Don't really know, Judge. I'd been ridin' and it woke me up. Didn't want to disturb Lucille and the boy so I went down to the office, told Ed Clyde he could take off — he's courtin' that li'l redhead from the Regal, you know her, Judge? Nice-lookin' . . . '

'Never mind the redhead, damnit, Waylon!' Getting edgy now.

'Well, I figured things were pretty quiet round town, it bein' a couple days till pay-day for them lumberjacks, but decided to check it out anyways. Locked up the office, Casey snorin' in his cell, and when I got back — hell, he'd gone.'

'Someone busted in?'

'Looked like it, Judge. Rear door's got pry-bar marks round the lock, wood frame splintered. Guess they took down the cell keys from the front office and let him out.'

Bligh pursed his flabby lips and let his several chins sink down on his upper chest. He folded his hands across his belly, looking down his large nose at the sheriff.

'You figure you'll catch up with 'em?'

'Reckon so, Judge. Already took a quick look downstream and found where they come outta the water. Got some men I volunteered for the posse. Ain't keen, but I figured if someone put up a small reward for Casey — '

'Not this someone. You lost him, you do it if you've a mind. I'm short of cash as it is. Damn mill swallows it like a well with a hole in the bottom.'

Dodge looked shocked. 'I can't afford no bounty, Judge. How about Lomas? He won't want Casey runnin' loose.'

' 'Spect not. But I sent a man out to Corey's soon as I heard about Casey's break-out. He might not put up a reward, but by hell, I'll bet he sends in Durango to help you out.' He leaned forward suddenly, wheezing. 'That don't please you, Waylon? Why, you look kinda put out . . . '

'I don't need them hardcases, Judge. I can handle this.'

'Not standing here gossiping, you can't.'

'Judge, you *sent* for me!'

'Well, you better go bring in this Casey and we can talk about the whys and wherefores later. Something not quite right here.'

'Why d'you say that?' Dodge's voice had a wavy edge to it now. He hoped the worry he felt didn't show on his face.

Bligh waved a large hand. 'Just go find him, Waylon — and if Durango shows up, you give him a free hand. That's an order.'

'Judge, *I*'m the sheriff — I oughta be in charge!'

Bligh merely stared, slowly rocking back and forth in his chair. Eventually Dodge nodded, set his hat on his head and went out and across the street to where his sleepy posse was waiting.

Man, if Durango bought into this, who knew what might happen . . .?

* * *

Butch Satterlee and Cotton Rix were no friendlier than they'd been the night before when they set out from the hidden camp on the grassy bench at the foot of Sawbuck Ridge in early morning. Casey, leading the way, surprised them.

He gave them a crooked smile. 'My land used to run right down there where that dry gulch is. Came up this way a few times just for the view, see how the land lay, figure what I could do with it once I'd proved up.'

'Mebbe Miz Ingram was right — you do know this neck of the woods better'n us,' opined Butch as Casey led them through tall timber, telling them it was a short cut to what was now Lomas's ranch.

They kept their eyes peeled for riders but saw none. Several cows grazed on the slopes and Casey wondered why there weren't more. When he asked, Rix said,

'Lomas is makin' more outta railroad ties than he can outta beef.'

'Which is why we figured to burn his trees.'

'It'd hit him hard,' admitted Casey, 'but maybe we can get him somewhere else he's not expecting.'

'Like where?' Satterlee demanded.

Casey didn't answer, but led the way out of the trees, across another small hogback rise and up to a flat ledge. He reined in — Dodge had even had his paint waiting at the jail — and pointed.

Far in the distance, just above the

riverbottoms, flat water glinted back at them, the sun striking glare off it as though from a mirror. It was almost a mile across, because the dam holding it back had been built across the narrow neck of a deep box-canyon which opened out like a bottle, very steep-sided.

Rix looked at Casey. 'Butch said it was no use tryin' to do anythin' to Lomas's dam. Wouldn't be worth it.'

Satterlee shrugged. 'Well, hell, what'll happen if we blow it? Water'll just run off through the old channel into the river, won't even flood. Be a waste of dynamite.'

'There's one helluva lot of water in there,' Casey said, impressed. 'Dam's much bigger than Lomas aimed to build originally. Why you think a dam has headgates, Butch?'

'So's they can control how much water they let go at one time.' Satterlee sounded smug: *hell, anyone knew that!*

'Yeah — *and* all that water is pushing against the main dam wall. What you reckon'd happen if it burst the gates?'

'Told you — water'll run through the old channel, into the river, way yonder.' Satterlee shook his head. 'It won't do much damage.'

'Then what're we even talkin' about it for?' growled Rix, impatiently.

'Boys, you gotta know your river and I made it my business to know this one — the part that ran through what used to be my land, leastways. Like right here.'

'Well, what about it? Hell, it's damn near the quietest section of the whole blame river!'

'Right — and quieter still with all this water dammed up, a few thousand gallons released through the headgates every day so as to take some of the strain off the wall. But if *all* that water was released at once, *all of it*, Butch, we'd have a roaring, whitewater flood that would sweep everything before it — including all those logs Lomas floats downstream from his land to Bligh's sawmill.'

He paused there, watching their faces as they saw the possibilities.

'Log jam!' breathed Rix, eyes lighting up. 'Big one!'

'Christ! It'd be *massive*!' Satterlee said happily. 'Big enough to flood the sawmill, float away all them ties they's cut, drown the donkey-engines, maybe make 'em explode . . . Holy Joe, it'd wreck the place, cost Bligh and Lomas every cent they've got!'

Casey nodded soberly. 'It's an idea, gents, ain't it. But we'll have to plan it carefully, don't want to drown the whole town. Lomas could have armed men at the dam, too. He knows what damage it could cause if it's blown up.'

'Well, first we gotta get our hands on some dynamite I reckon,' Butch said.

'I know where,' Rix offered, excitement showing on his moon face now. 'They got some in that line camp of Lomas's up near Potluck Ridge, usin' it to blow down them big red oaks. Only thing is, there's six men workin' outta that camp, sometimes more.'

Butch swore, but after a short silence, Casey said,

'Well, we'll just have to shorten the odds.'

* * *

Corey Lomas and Judge Bligh were waiting in the latter's office, sipping good bonded whiskey, when Durango came in without knocking. Bligh was about to admonish him for the oversight but when he saw the man's face he bit off the words before they were spoken.

'What'd you find?' Lomas asked.

Durango had been sent down to the jail to look things over. He walked to the sideboy, helped himself to a large slug of the expensive whiskey and tossed it down before facing the men. But apparently he liked the taste, for he turned back and poured another glassful, taking a sip before speaking.

Judge Bligh asked sourly. 'Like a drink?'

'Got one, Judge,' Durango said, unperturbed, indicating his glass. 'Boss, no one busted into that jail — leastways not through the rear door.'

Both men sat up straight. 'Dodge said there were pry-bar marks,' Lomas said and Durango nodded, sipping again.

'There are — all round the part of the doorframe near the lock.'

'Well?' Bligh snapped, wheezing as usual. 'Then someone broke in!'

Durango almost smiled. 'Judge — the lock was *un*locked, you know what I mean?'

They frowned, not understanding.

'Boss, if that door was locked so someone had to use a pry-bar to get in, then the lock itself ought to be — *locked* right? The tongue solid, not able to move in its slot . . . Think about it for a minute . . . But that tongue was goin' in and out of the body of the lock, no problem at all.'

They saw it then.

'The damn thing was unlocked all

the time, the pry-bar marks were added to make it look like someone busted in,' Lomas said. The judge swore, swore louder when he spilled some of his whiskey down his vest.

'By Godfrey! You saying Waylon deliberately left it unlocked?'

'Think I oughta ride out and find him and ask him, Judge, don't you?'

Durango gulped down the rest of his whiskey and smacked his lips as he looked from one man to the other.

Then he turned and refilled his glass.

No one objected.

9

Dead By Sundown

Heading back to their camp on the grassy bench in the draw, Butch growled, 'Why the hell don't we go get that dynamite now?'

Casey smiled thinly. 'Like the idea of blowing the dam now, eh, Butch?'

'If we're gonna do it, let's get it done.'

Cotton Rix agreed. 'Might's well.'

'You fellers know how to set dynamite? So's you can light it without blowing your own head off, I mean. Right place to put it around the headgates . . . ?'

They murmured and Satterlee spat but said nothing coherent by way of an answer.

'Thought so. Well, I've handled dynamite before. Had a job at a mine once, big copper company, and they made us all go to lectures on safety in handling and planting charges. I'll fix the charges on the dam so we don't send the whole shebang down all at once and wipe out Keystone and likely every ranch between the dam-site and the town. We only want to get at Lomas and Bligh, not the whole county.'

They were passing through a draw and suddenly Butch reined down, hauled his mount around and rammed it into Casey's smaller paint. The horse whinnied and slipped on the rough ground at the edge of the trail. Rix hesitated a moment, drove his horse forward while Casey was still off-balance and slammed into the paint, too. The Indian pony went down, thrashing, throwing Casey.

Butch Satterlee bared his teeth in a tight grin of pleasure, spurred his horse forward as Casey started to get up out of the dust. He hurled himself aside as Butch rushed by and Rix was still making up his mind just how deeply he was going to get involved in this when Casey reached up and yanked him out of the saddle.

The man gave a startled yell as Casey twisted, using Rix's own body momentum, and hurled him into the thick brush. Rix bounced off and fell heavily amongst rocks where he lay gasping.

Satterlee had turned his mount now and started to lunge it back when Casey's sixgun jumped into his hand. Butch hauled rein fast, almost pulling the horse up on to its rear legs.

'Whoa!' he shouted, and he wasn't addressing the horse now. 'Hold up a minute!'

With the reins drawn tightly, he lifted his free hand as Casey lined up his cocked pistol on him. He held his fire — but only just.

'The hell's wrong with you?' Casey demanded, angrily.

Butch glared but was still wary. 'Listen, I run things here! You come bouncin' in and try to take over. Well, I ain't gonna stand for it!'

'Christ, is that all? You didn't like me saying I'd plant the dynamite at the dam? You're a blamed fool, Butch. I'm trying to save your life. But Margarita Ingram told me you'd rather talk than fight any time, so . . . .' Casey leathered the Colt, spread his hands. 'You want to get this outta your gall right now?'

It took Butch by surprise but with hardly any hesitation at all he jammed home his spurs and his horse jumped at Casey, sending the man sprawling as he dived aside. Butch was out of the saddle in a flash, sliding down on top of Casey, slamming three hard punches into the back of his neck and shoulders, hauling him on to his back, rearing up, preparing to stomp on him.

Casey, dazed, fighting by instinct, caught the descending boot in both hands, twisted hard, and Butch yelled as he was flung sprawling, sliding across the grass. Casey dived after him, somersaulted and rolled to his feet as the groggy Satterlee lurched up. Casey hammered him with a barrage of blows to the body and two to the head that put the big man down, spitting blood and a broken tooth.

Raging, eyes wild with fury, he came thrusting up, swinging. Casey stepped back, felt the wind of a haymaker passing his jaw, blocked the next blow on his forearm, feeling his muscles creak as he parried. He stepped in with one leg between Butch's and clubbed a fist down into his face. Satterlee's knees buckled and Casey danced to one side, thrust out three blurring lefts — *one, two, three!* — followed with a looping right that put Butch down where he sat, shaking his head, watching drops of his blood spray across the rich green of the grass. It was so lush and springy that Casey didn't hear Cotton Rix coming up behind, swinging his sixgun by the barrel.

But Butch saw him and flung a handful of twigs into Rix's face. Casey ducked, was startled to hear Rix grunt and slip as he staggered back, dropping his gun.

'He's mine!' growled Satterlee, pushing all the way up and launching himself bodily at Casey.

Casey dropped flat and Butch sailed over him, trying to twist in mid-air, dropped awkwardly and winded himself against a rock. Casey swung towards him, pulled him to a sitting position by his shirtfront and rammed two short-armed but devastating blows against his jaw. Butch's head snapped back and he went slack. Casey hit him once more and let him drop.

Rix was picking up his gun but when he heard Casey's Colt slide out of leather he let it fall to the grass, lifted both hands.

'Don't shoot!'

Casey motioned for him to stay put and found a deadfall to sit on, nursing the sixgun, sweat and a little blood dripping from his face as he watched both men, letting his breathing settle.

'Butch just likes — to do things — his way,' Rix gasped.

'I'm just trying to convince him that

all I want to do is nail Lomas and Bligh,' Casey said wearily.

'Think — you mighta — done it,' Rix allowed as he watched his pard slowly sit up, rubbing his jaw and running a tongue gingerly around inside his cut mouth.

Butch still had plenty of hate in his eyes but there was a noticeable wariness there, too, as he looked at Casey.

'This don't settle nothin'!' he growled and Casey sighed, lifting his hands and letting them fall again, limply, as much as to say, *I give up . . .*

Casey stood somewhat stiffly, rubbing one leg down the side above the knee. 'You two go on back to your camp. I'll scout around, take a look at that line camp up Potluck Ridge, see how many men are there, then check out the dam. We'll work out a plan tonight okay?'

As he climbed up the slope to where his paint now stood, browsing on the lush grass, Butch glared after him and said quietly,

'There he goes again. Tryin' to take over.'

'Well, I dunno, Butch,' Rix said just as quietly. 'I ain't too keen to handle dynamite. Never done it, if you want to know.'

'Don't want to know and don't care.' Satterlee's gaze followed Casey as the man rode away without looking in their direction, heading for Potluck Ridge. 'You do like I say and you'll be all right.'

'What we gonna do now?'

'I'm gonna go back and brew some coffee and take me a rest — that son of a bitch packs a punch like a Missouri mule.'

Maybe there was a faint hint of respect in his gravelly voice.

Just a hint . . .

* * *

Durango took Woody and Pidge with him — not that he needed them, but seeing as there were six in Dodge's posse you just never knew. Long Frank and Baldy Reems were nursing their broken noses and shattered teeth and likely wouldn't be much good for anything for some days.

By that time, with any luck, Casey would be dead.

They picked up the posse on the way back from searching downstream. Dodge didn't seem too happy to see them, especially when Durango said:

'Killed enough time down here? Takin' 'em back to look where Casey really went now?'

The posse men looked at one another, not savvying this, but they savvied the hard looks Pidge and Woody gave them, hands resting on their rifles across their thighs. Waylon Dodge composed his face, frowning.

'Tracks came out of the creek behind the law office downstream, so that's the place we started searchin'. Tryin' upstream now, because — '

'Because you've wasted enough time,' cut in Durango harshly. 'Waylon, you're in trouble.'

'Mebbe you're the one in trouble if you figure on stoppin' an official posse goin' about its duty,' Dodge snapped but there wasn't as much bite to it as he would have liked.

Durango grinned, cold enough to send a shiver through most of the posse.

'Well, that might be, but like I said, you've just been wastin' time so as to give Casey a chance to get away. Who'd you get to bust him out? Them two old daisies from back in the hills? Satterlee and Rix?'

The posse men were mighty uneasy now and someone among them muttered, 'Reckon we oughta head back to town.'

Dodge snapped his head around. 'You stay put!'

'No,' Durango contradicted him. 'That's a good idea. You boys head on back. Search is over. I'm takin' charge now — on Judge Bligh's say-so.'

He nodded to Woody and Pidge and they closed on the nervous posse-men, waving their rifles. The townsmen took little urging and started away down the trail, the two hardcases riding a little behind them.

Durango folded his big, brutal hands on his saddle horn, watching Dodge, deciding whether to accept this or make a stand.

He had no real choice, not if he wanted to keep on wearing that sheriff's star.

'Listen, Durango, I'm the sheriff! I'm in charge of any posse — I don't give a damn what Judge Bligh told you, I'm the law in this county and — '

'Waylon — shut up.' When Dodge stopped in mid-sentence, his jaw hanging slackly, Durango said tiredly, 'Dunno what's wrong with your hearin' — I said I'm takin' over. Already done it by sendin' the posse home. See, there's a new posse now — Woody, Pidge, you and me. We'll find this Casey ourselves. 'Cause you know where he is.'

'The hell you sayin' . . . ?'

'Shut-*up*, Waylon! Christ, you gonna

keep up this pretence you didn't leave that rear door unlocked and later put the pry-bar marks on the frame? Just don't try to gimme no more twaddle! You do and I'll kill you right here.'

The words froze Waylon Dodge. *Right here* . . . like, *instead of later, somewhere else* . . .

Either way he knew for sure now that he was a dead man. Unless . . .

He let his shoulders slump as if he was beaten and was going to co-operate, then, anxious to get this done before Woody and Pidge came back, he sighed resignedly and straightened in the saddle.

Durango was still leaning on his hands folded across his saddle horn.

Suddenly, Dodge's right hand swept down to his sixgun in what was probably the fastest draw he'd ever made.

Or would make . . .

His eyes bulged wide open as the first of Durango's bullets punched into his chest and started him rolling back out of the saddle. *Unbelievable! No one was that fast!*

Before his body hit the ground, Durango had shot him four more times. He was reloading when Woody and Pidge came riding in, followed hesitantly by three of the posse-men.

They all stared at the sheriff's body.

'Turned mean on me.' Durango managed to sound both mystified and offended. 'Because the judge sent me down to take over. Mighty touchy feller, old Waylon. Had to defend myself, didn't I?'

Even the posse-men nodded slowly, swallowing.

'Well, now you're here, you might's well take him back to town. Woody, Pidge and me've got a chore to do. Let's go, boys, I want to see Casey dead by sundown.'

* * *

Butch Satterlee and Cotton Rix rested up at the camp, both going to sleep, maybe dreaming of what they would do to Casey once he had served his purpose.

It was Margarita Ingram who woke them, riding hell-bent into the hideout, calling their names as she spurred her sweat-sheened mount up the slope and across the grassy bench. She was quitting the saddle when the men blinked and stumbled off their bedrolls in their lean-tos, rubbing their eyes.

If she noticed the signs of recent fighting she didn't take time to mention it.

'Where's Casey?' she demanded breathlessly.

'Who cares?' murmured Rix.

Satterlee squinted. 'Casey? Dunno. What's more, don't care.'

'Well, you'd better start caring, both of you!' The girl lashed at them with the quirt that dangled from her right wrist, slashing across their shoulders and the arms they instinctively raised over their heads for protection. 'I want to know where Casey is!'

Butch Satterlee grabbed her wrist and squeezed, hurting her deliberately as he pulled her in close, teeth gritted behind his split lips.

'Don't ever take a whip to me again, woman, or I'll snap your neck like a reed!'

His free hand wrapped strong fingers around her slender throat and gave a squeeze that widened her eyes and brought her up on to her toes. He shook her and released her. She rubbed at her neck, watching him warily.

'Now, what's your hurry to find Casey?'

'Durango has killed Waylon Dodge,' she said, fighting to clear her throat.

That got their attention and Rix shrugged, spat.

'Not much loss far as I'm concerned.'

'Nor me,' agreed Satterlee and Margarita curled a lip disdainfully.

'Don't either of you have any common sense at all? Can't you think of anything else but yourselves?'

'Sure,' Butch answered. 'We think

about Lomas and how we're gonna wreck everythin' he's worked for with that damn Judge Bligh.'

She placed her hands on her hips, shaking her head slowly. 'Don't you see what's happening? Now Waylon is dead there's no official law here. It won't surprise me if Judge Bligh appoints Durango as the next sheriff. *Then* where will you be? Where will any of us be?'

The men had enough sense to see what she was saying and Rix scratched at his head, looked at Butch for guidance.

'Well, if Dodge is dead, ain't anythin' we can do about that,' Satterlee said finally.

'No, but we can make sure Durango never gets to wear the star. I have to tell Casey about this!'

'Yeah, guess so. Well, he was gonna check out the Potluck Ridge line camp and then he said he was goin' down to the dam.'

She started. 'The — dam?'

'So he said.' Butch threw a warning glance at Rix, telling him not to say anything about the plan to blow it up. 'Wants to see how many men Lomas has, I guess.'

'He only had to ask me. Or *you* could've told him. You've been harassing Lomas for a long time . . . '

Butch shrugged, touching his fresh black eye and battered mouth. 'Case and me ain't been seein' eye to eye you might say lately. He wanted to find out for himself.'

'You'd better saddle up and ride with me.'

'Not us. We're goin' our way, Casey's goin' his,' Satterlee told her.

She flicked her gaze to Rix and he shrugged, going along with his pard. Margarita's jaw firmed.

'We had a deal! I've let you dance around, not really doing much harm to Lomas, just waiting for a chance to move in and do something that'll wipe him out! I've supplied you with food and bullets and mounts and even a couple of women, once. It's time to settle up. Casey's here and he has the biggest grudge you can think of against Lomas and Bligh. We have to use him! You *have* to get along with him! At least until he's — unleashed on Lomas.'

Satterlee was shaking his head before she had finished speaking.

'We'll do this our way.'

'You fool! Casey has a conscience, he's one of those men who live by a strict code. Dodge went out on a limb for him by arranging that jailbreak, now Durango's killed Dodge. If I know Casey he'll go after Durango and then lash out at Corey Lomas and Judge Bligh so they'll think the world is turning upside down — '

'Do what you want,' Satterlee said stubbornly. 'Cotton an' me've got a couple chores of our own to do.'

He felt a small thrill of fear for just a moment, the way she looked at him, before wheeling her mount and riding off, lashing with the quirt.

Rix blew out his cheeks. 'What chores, Butch?'

'Gonna blow the dam ain't we?'

'Well, yeah, but Casey's gonna show us how to handle the dynamite first.'

'What's to handlin' it? You stick in the detonator an' light the fuse. Anyway, Casey's outta this. It's just you an' me now.'

'But — we don't have the dynamite yet.'

Butch leered. 'We will — before sundown, too.'

'Hey, wait up! We don't even know how many men are in that line camp.'

'We soon will. I know how we can just walk in and take what we want, no matter how many Lomas has got workin' there. Now get your goddamn guns and your saddle and *let's go!*'

10

Mantracks

Casey was stretched out in the long grass on a knoll, looking down at the dam. Lomas hadn't built it in the original position he had planned on. Or, least-ways, the one he had told Casey and everyone else about before Casey had started out on the trail drive.

It was supposed to be on a branch of the main river stream, the ground rising slightly to a narrow gap between two walls of a box canyon. The idea had been to blow some rocks down into the gap, then build the dam on top, raising it just enough to take headgates. Cheap but effective.

Instead, and maybe once he had the money from the sale of those stolen cattle, and access to land that had been Casey's, Lomas had chosen a place upstream, with a bigger canyon fed by mountain streams and had ended up with this man-made lake.

He had thought earlier that the position was not the one he had been expecting but Satterlee and Rix tended to command a man's attention with their griping and trying to make sure they ran things their way. *The Good Lord help us if ever that happened!*

Now he adjusted the focus on the field glasses with a cracked lens that tended to throw one image atop the other without either one being complete. He had taken them from Satterlee's saddle-bags and wasn't surprised that they were in such condition, knowing the man's slovenly habits. But it was enough to see that there was a lone guard — taking it easy, too, dozing, looked like — up on the north side near the gear for raising the headgates.

Man, there was a lot of water behind that log-and-rubble wall, constantly fed by those streams. Blow that wall and you could say *adios* to half of Lomas's ranch, the sawmill and most of Keystone. Unfortunately, it would be mostly houscs that would be swept away, families of the men who worked at the sawmill which seemed to go twenty-four hours a day. He reckoned that was earning your money the hard way, never out of earshot of the mill, night or day . . .

He lowered the lenses to the headgates. Bigger than he reckoned on, they would take more dynamite than he had thought, but it could still be done without disturbing the main wall. Water would gush out at a rate of thousands of gallons a minute, but if the whole wall went . . .

Well, he'd read about huge tidal waves that swept in from the oceans every so often, wiping out entire cities, travelling many miles inland before losing their power.

He nodded to himself as he picked out where he would place the charges so as to dislodge the gates. All he needed to do was jump them out of the frame. Water was already leaking, which was normal enough, so there would be ready-made hollows to take the charges. Use a little pitch at the point where the fuse entered the stick, attached to the detonator, so it didn't get swamped and —

'You should hide your horse better. I saw it from way down the slope.'

He twisted, dropping the glasses, sixgun coming up, the hammer cocked, ready to shoot. But he held his fire as he saw the pale, startled face of Margarita Ingram crouching beside a rock at the edge of the patch of long grass. Fear flared in her eyes and she raised one small, gloved hand.

'Don't!' she whispered.

But he had already lowered the hammer although he kept the gun pointing at her.

'You move as quiet as smoke.' He grinned as he saw her face. 'I meant that as a compliment. Nearly got yourself shot, though.'

'Would you have fired?' she asked a little shakily, sitting down against the rock. 'With that guard up by the headgates?'

'Yeah, if I'd figured I was gonna get shot if I didn't.'

She smiled. 'Well, my heart's still trying to settle down. That was the fastest draw I've ever seen! And from a lying down posiiton!' When he said nothing, she asked, 'Where did you learn that?'

Sliding the gun back into the holster, he said, 'It's a talent a man is born with — needs honing and practice to keep it or improve it, though.'

'Well, I'd say you practise a lot.' As that brought no response, she added, 'Butch said I'd probably find you up here.'

'What brings you?'

'Bad news, I'm afraid — Durango has killed Waylon Dodge.'

Casey frowned, watching her. She gave him what sketchy details she knew, told by the posse-men who had brought in his body. They had stopped at her ranch on the way back to town for coffee and grub, no one liking the thought of having to give Mrs Dodge the bad news.

'So no one knows if Dodge was given a fair shakes or not,' observed Casey.

'Durango has a reputation for being very fast on the draw.'

'Waylon was no slacker, as I recall.'

'Apparently he wasn't good enough — or, as you suggest, he could have been murdered in cold blood. Knowing Durango, I think that's what probably happened. On Lomas's orders, of course. He got rid of all witnesses first, then . . . ' She shook her head lowering her eyes. 'Poor Lucille — and that little boy . . . '

Casey nodded, but it was obvious his thoughts were elsewhere.

'Durango is searching for you — with Pidge and Woody. I thought I'd better warn you.'

Casey snapped his head up. 'You know where they are?'

'Travelling upstream according to the posse-men. I imagine they think you'll be looking over Lomas's spread.' She sighed, teeth tugging at her lower lip. 'I can't help thinking about Waylon's wife and child. Lucille was never very popular. Even though she's Bligh's niece, she doesn't deserve this sort of thing. Waylon loved that boy, now he'll have to grow up without a father . . . '

'Happens, unfortunately. And I'd better move from here.'

'Where're you going?'

'Might travel downstream a ways, cross over to the far bank and lay a few tracks into that wild country over there.'

She smiled faintly, eyes bright. 'You're going to lay an ambush for Durango and the others!'

'See how it works out. And you? Where're you going?'

She looked mildly surprised. 'Why — back to my ranch of course. Where did you think I'd be going?'

'Maybe into town — see what you

can do for Lucille Dodge and the boy . . . ?'

She was already sliding backwards. Maybe she didn't hear him.

She didn't answer, anyway.

* * *

Durango liked to tell folk that he had a touch of Apache blood in him and that was what made him such a good tracker.

'Gran'mother was raped by an Apache warrior when a wagon train was attacked south of Tucson, Arizona. She died givin' birth to my ma, who looked more Mexican than anythin' else. But she got shoved on to the San Carlos reservation for a spell after I was borne. Dunno who my father was — so I grew up with men who'd rode with Vittorio, one even went back far as Mangus Colorada, Old Red Sleeves, or Red Shirt, they sometimes called him. So, I learned from the best trackers the world's ever seen or is likely to see.'

No one paid him much mind because he always told the story in an arrogant manner, hoping to provoke an insult from one of the listencrs, but Durango had demonstrated he wasn't boasting idly on several occasions.

And this was one of them.

They picked up man-tracks on the south side of the river, leading off into the wildest part of the hills.

'Guess he's not gonna bother Corey after all,' opined Woody but wished he had kept his mouth shut when he caught the look Durango threw him.

'That what you think, huh? How about you, Pidge?'

The man shrugged. 'Could look that way.'

'You mean, you dunno, but too scared to say so. Pair of dummies. By now, Casey's got the word Dodge is dead. He was friends with that stupid sheriff. I know Casey's type. He'll want to come after me, square things. But he ain't fool enough to brace me on the ranch. So he leads me away.'

'Judas!' breathed Woody, unsheathing his rifle and looking about him at the heavy timber and rugged, rock-studded slopes. 'He'll be layin' for us then!'

Pidge swore and looked a mite pale as he reached for his own rifle. Durango, squatting by the tracks, shook his head slowly and stood up.

'Dunno why I brought you pair. Sure, he'll be layin' for us, but not here. He'll pick the place and it'll give him all the advantage.'

'We go get some more men?' Pidge asked anxiously and Durango scowled.

'Always figured you had a yaller streak.' He wasn't worried that Pidge might take offence: what could the man do against someone like Durango? Hell, he could eat up a dozen Pidges and not even bother to spit out the bones.

'What we do . . . ' Durango paused and raked them with his bleak eyes. 'What we do is, we separate. I ride on, followin' the tracks the way he wants. You two ride parallel with me, one either side, close enough to see where

I'm headed but not close enough so's Casey'll know it. I'll signal, take off my hat and blot my face with my *left* shirt sleeve. My *left* arm, okay? That means go to ground, let me get ahead and then circle out so's you can get ahead of me and come up behind Casey — '

'How'll we know where he is?' *Woody, the dumb bastard, of course . . .*

'*I*'ll know where he is. I'll drop back so you can get ahead and nail him in a crossfire while he's expectin' me to ride into a headshot. Think you can savvy that or will I say it all over again?'

They didn't look happy, but Pidge and Woody said they knew what to do.

'Good. Now let's see if we can still see Casey dead by sundown!'

As they prepared to separate, Pidge asked, 'What we do if you use your *right* arm, Durango?'

Jesus! 'I *won't* use my right arm — I keep that for my gun. *Now* you got it?'

'I — I guess so.'

Durango shook his head. He had an urge to shoot them both and tell Lomas

Casey had nailed them . . .

By God, he might do that yet.

* * *

Durango's signal came earlier than they expected.

They were spread out in the pattern, Durango following the man-tracks, Pidge on his left, moving cautiously through brush on a small rise about fifty yards off. Woody was on Durango's right, a little closer because the country was rugged here, full of corkscrew dry-washes and scattered brush.

Suddenly Durango straightened from where he had been examining a recent chip off a flat rock, just curved enough to make a man think it had been made by a careless horseshoe. The hardcase smiled grimly to himself, swept off his hat with his left hand and used the same arm to blot sweat from his forehead on his shirt. The signal.

He set his hat on the back of his head, casual, showing either disdain or raw guts by standing there making a target of himself for the man he knew was waiting only thirty yards away, drawing a bead on him even at this moment.

No shot came and Durango figured Pidge and Woody ought to be in position by now. *He hoped like hell they were!* Because he could see Casey — well, he could see the man's hat, or part of it, showing through a screen of brush and there was a straight line that just had to be the man's rifle.

But he hadn't seen *him*! The man hadn't moved, yet Durango was standing here, giving him first shot . . .

He jumped when he heard the scream.

Off to his left, cut short, no other sound. But his skin rippled with goosebumps and he dropped to one knee, sweeping his sixgun out of leather, heart pounding as he looked around.

It was already too late for Pidge. He lay sprawled amongst the rocks, his throat cut, blood glistening against the rock where he had holed up, hoping to draw a bead on Casey.

The man in buckskin was moving like a ghost now, hatless, bloody blade still in his hand, passing from rock to rock with no more noise than a shadow. In the brush he went belly down, writhing forward with only the faintest of sounds made by his buckskin skimming the earth.

'I see him, Durango!'

He recognized Woody's voice, just ahead, glimpsed the man standing now amongst brush-screened rock, rifle to shoulder. Casey rolled swiftly down slope as the first bullets raked through his cover, spitting into the hard earth, kicking small, clattering chunks against his rolling body.

The knife slid into the beaded sheath Stone Man had given him and his Colt came up. As he slid past a gap in the brush he triggered and his bullet ricocheted from the rock in front of Woody. The man reared back, stumbling, and Casey snatched a brush-root, halting his slide, triggered two quick shots. Woody shuddered and swayed for a moment before toppling forward and crashing down the slope, loose-limbed and dead before he came to a stop.

Casey hurled himself backwards as he heard the faint click of a gun hammer cocking. Then there were hammering shots as lead raked the brush. Durango had spotted him now — *really* spotted him and not just the hat and stick he had set up on the ridge. Casey rode up on his knees, chopped at his gun hammer, getting off two more shots, more or less just to let Durango know he had a fight on his hands, then hurled himself bodily into the rocks. He lay awkwardly, shucking shells from his gunbelt, replacing the used ones in his Colt's cylinder.

They didn't waste breath shouting at each other: they were here to kill and each knew why. Just as they knew only one was going to ride away from this slope.

Casey didn't know where Durango was now. The man was good — maybe that story about him being part-Apache wasn't just eyewash after all. He had the urge to move but fought it down: it was dangerous when the enemy could be only yards away, invisible in the thicker brush, just waiting for your nerve to crack. And the moment you made a move — it would be your last.

A man needed patience, something Casey had learned over the years.

Durango likely knew it, too, but the man was so arrogant, so eager to kill that maybe he would be the one to make the first — and last — mistake.

Slowly, an inch at a time, Casey drew up his right leg, bending it carefully beneath him. Then, using the same deliberate action, he changed his body position so that he was sitting now on both bent legs, giving him a couple of inches more height. When he turned his head he did so in a smooth but sluggish movement, eyes sweeping the slope, pinched down against the glare, checking every twig and leaf — and the small spaces in between.

Sweat trickled down his face, hung on his set jaw, ran down his dirt-smeared neck and on to his chest. It gathered in his eyebrows and he blinked when it dammed up to the point where it spilled over into his eye-sockets. It stung his eyes and he almost missed Durango as he blinked furiously, using tears to deaden the stinging and help clear his vision.

There! A flash of blue that he momentarily thought was a small butterfly — there were several flitting about here despite the drifting gun-smoke. Durango was wearing a blue shirt — and *the man was below him*!

Something Casey hadn't expected. It was only that he was instinctively moving his head in a one-hundred-eighty-degree arc and happened to glance downhill that he saw the killer.

Now was the time to move and move fast!

His Colt came up. He snapped a shot and somersaulted over the rocks, landing awkwardly on the slope, his feet going out from under him, taking him down towards the killer. But Durango spun around with the strike of Casey's lead and his gun blazed as the man slid towards him. Bullets tore up the slope around Casey's moving body and then he was past, firing again, hearing the lead ricochet, but seeing Durango claw at his face. *Rock chips or pieces of lead*, he thought, as he jarred into brush and a short broken twig gouged across his ribs and snapped off in his flesh. The pain was worse than a bullet as the wood splintered and he doubled over, groping for support, knowing he was well within Durango's line of fire now.

Durango was hit, high in the chest, but off to one side, likely only a muscle torn up some. His face was streaked with blood but the man was very much alive and he bared his teeth as he pointed his Colt at Casey and fired. The lead went so close it lifted the long hair that Casey used to cover the bald patch above his ear. He felt a sting on top of his ear and knew death had passed him with barely a half-inch to spare.

He didn't aim to waste his second chance, yanked the broken twig from his side with a gasping grunt and twisted as another bullet tore into the space, missing again. But he landed belly down and jabbed his elbows into the ground, glimpsed Durango's startled, unbelieving face as he looked into the smoking muzzle of the Colt and squeezed the trigger.

Durango's head snapped back, the big body jerked and rolled sideways and slowly his legs straightened. Casey kept him covered, even though the man's face had been virtually destroyed by his bullet, walked forward and kicked the sixgun well out of reach.

Not necessary, of course: not even a man like Durango could get up after taking a slug through the middle of the face.

'That was for Reno as well as Waylon Dodge,' Casey said quietly, kneeling beside the man.

He was reaching for Durango's bloody shirt front when he paused, sniffing. *Smoke!*

He climbed up on a rock so he could see better and there it was, rolling and twisting into the afternoon sky at a place he thought was in the direction of . . .

'Potluck Ridge!' he said aloud. 'The line camp — and those stupid sons of bitches have set the hills on fire!'

11

Fire

'I counted seven,' said Cotton Rix.

'I know there were eight the other day,' answered Butch Satterlee.

They were both lying sprawled on a ridge over-looking the work area of the men who were living in the line camp on Potluck Ridge. These were experienced lumberjacks brought in by Corey Lomas and Judge Bligh. They were felling trees, stripping them of branches, and when they had sufficient logs ready they would send for Lomas's cowhands to do the donkey-work. This would entail hitching chains to the felled logs and dragging them to the slope that had been cleared down to the river, rolling the logs down into the water where the current would eventually sweep them down to the mill at Keystone.

There was a water-chute planned, to come in from the dam, dog-leg across the slopes to this area. Then the logs could be dropped into the wooden chute raised on trestles and the rushing water released from the dam on demand would carry them to the river.

The cowhands reckoned that day couldn't come fast enough. Several had quit, griping that they were still on ranch hand's pay but were expected to do this heavy, dangerous work of dragging logs down steep slopes to the treacherous waters of the Big Bad River.

Lomas didn't try to keep the quitters: he could have offered a small rise in pay but he merely told them to collect their gear and be off the place before sundown of that day.

The others stayed, simply because there were plenty of men waiting in Keystone to take their place. A lot of men were coming in to the boom town, finding most jobs taken, ready to work for low wages just so they could survive until something better came along — if it ever did.

Butch and Rix had had to crawl closer than they really wanted to because Casey had Butch's field glasses, the only ones they possessed.

They lay there, still watching the men, axes glittering in the sun as they swung them expertly in overcuts and undercuts, eating into the wood, chips and sap flying, the honed blades making short work of even the biggest trees.

The noise of the felled giants was deafening as they toppled, taking down shorter trees, splintering branches as thick as a man's thigh, leaves and twigs flying with clouds of dust.

The felled trees had hardly settled, some still actually bouncing a little before the men swarmed over them, slicing off branches, trimming them down so the men at the mill could haul them directly from the river and feed them into the endlessly singing saws. The men were plastered with layers of sawdust and sticky sap, in their hair, stiffening their clothes, stinging their skin and eyes. Any man who had the sap squirt into his eyes immediately thunked his axe blade into the tree — *never* into the ground or even dropping it on to the ground — and then he would run to a keg of water lashed to a small sled nearby, plunge his head and face in. Many a lumberjack who had neglected to wash the raw sap from his eyes had ended up half-or all the way blind.

So the place was full of movement and action and noise. Which meant the two watchers had little to worry about: they could talk, cough, move about — carefully — without worrying too much about being detected by the busy men below.

'I still reckon one man's missin',' Satterlee said.

'Well, what difference does it make? There's too many for us to tackle, Butch.'

Satterlee gave him a sardonic look. 'I

said we're gonna get that dynamite by sundown and that's what we're gonna do.'

Rix shook his head. 'Count me out. I ain't goin' up agin all those *hombres* — '

'You see any guns?'

'No, but — '

'Ah, don't matter. Come with me. I'll show you how we're gonna get the dynamite.'

Rix wasn't sure about this, but he hadn't seen Butch so confident or decisive before, so figured the man must have a plan that would work — or one he believed would.

They slid back down to where they had ground-hitched their horses in a hollow, and mounted. Rix was glad to be riding away from this place but instead of turning towards the trail between the hills that would take them to their hideout, Satterlee led the way into a draw that brought them out amidst stands of heavy timber and brush growth. Rix figured it would be a little higher than the lumber camp and likely a mile or two distant. It was hard to tell with all the twisting and climbing they had done.

His belly tightened when Butch called a halt and dismounted.

'C'mon — get down. We got work to do.'

Rix frowned, looking around him, smelling the resins and scents of the trees and brush-flowers, seeing and hearing the birds that flitted about, spotting a chipmunk and what he believed was a squirrel streaking for cover.

'What we doin' here? Aw, Judas, Butch, *no*!'

This last protest came when he saw Satterlee taking old rags and a bottle of coal-oil from his saddle-bags. Butch barely glanced at Rix as he uncapped the bottle and soaked the rags.

'Toss 'em around some of the brush while I pile this lot against the tree,' Butch ordered.

'The whole damn hills'll go up in smoke!'

'Who gives a damn? Trees burned are trees Lomas and Bligh can't make a profit from.'

'But — it might reach the town!'

Butch looked up from placing his rags, one hand feeling for vestas in his shirt pocket. His face was grim.

'Keystone folk ever do you any favours?'

'No, but — aw, hell!'

The vesta flared into flame and a moment later the rags caught. The fire licked at the bark of the tree and the grass at its base. Rix resignedly took his oil-soaked rags and tossed them into some brush. He picked up a clump of burning grass and threw it after the rags.

In minutes the heat had driven them back, causing the horses to snort and roll their eyes. They rode away swiftly, ears already ringing with the crackle of the brush and whipcracks of sap blowing pieces of bark out of the burning tree-trunks.

* * *

They reined in below the level of the fire which was already leaping into a red wall, smoke roiling against the pale blue of the sky. They could hear the yelling of the lumberjacks and in minutes the men were arriving, some with axes, others with sacking, three men dragging the water-butt on its wooden sled, lid in place to prevent too much spillage.

Others manhandled the sled closer to the fire, ripped off the cover and soaked the sacks. Men snatched them, dripping, ran to the base of the trees and brush, swiping at the fires with the wet sacks.

'They know what to do!' Rix exclaimed, throat raw from the swirling smoke.

'They'll need a hundred men to put that out,' Satterlee said with grim satisfaction. 'Like to stay and watch but we got us some dynamite to collect. Let's go.'

* * *

Satterlee was right: there was an eighth man.

He was in the cabin of the line camp, a substantial log-and-riverstone affair that could sleep a dozen men comfortably and had plenty of room for stores of all kinds, whether it be food or work-gear. Or explosives.

Rix said that from what he had heard, the dynamite was kept in a specially built room at one end of the cabin, double-planked, lined with sheet-iron to protect the explosives inside. There was a big iron lock on the door.

'So we gotta get in that cabin, Butch.'

'Get that goddamn whine outa your voice before I stick a knife in you!' snapped Satterlee and Rix knew Butch was as much on edge as he was now they had seen the man moving about the cabin.

He was using crutches and when he came to the door to look up the slope at the spreading fire through a pair of field glasses, Satterlee lifted his rifle and shot him through the chest. The man tumbled back into the cabin, the crutch falling, his bandaged leg resting on the stoop. Rix silently followed Butch down and they were within ten yards of the door when the bandaged leg was drawn inside and the door swung shut.

'You didn't kill him!' Rix exclaimed needlessly.

They knew the wounded man couldn't move around much and Satterlee went to a window near the door where the shutter was propped outwards with a short length of timber. He had started to lift the shutter with one hand when a gun blazed from inside and he wrenched away, yelling, clapping a hand to his face, dropping his rifle. A sliver of wood torn from the frame by the bullet had pierced his cheek and hung from his face, dripping blood.

Cotton Rix used his head for once, crouched as he ran to the cabin wall, rose and flattened against the logs, looking sideways through the gap between the propped shutter and the frame of another window. He saw the wounded man lying where he had fallen, just inside the door, his bandaged foot almost against the planks. He had a smoking Colt in his hands, saw Rix and fired.

Cotton dropped to a crouch again, ran to the door and kicked it in. There was a scream of pain from inside as the door smashed into the man's bandaged foot. Rix stumbled inside, kicked the gun from the man's hand and placed the rifle muzzle against his head.

Satterlee came in, clutching the bloody splinter he had wrenched from his face.

'Not yet!' he yelled as Rix's finger tightened on the trigger. He stood over the wounded man and bared his teeth, leaning down. 'Where's the key to the dynamite room?'

The man, in obvious pain, shook his head.

'Hopin' you'd do that,' Butch said, turned and kicked viciously at the injured foot.

The man screamed and convulsed, blood trickling from a corner of his mouth now. His eyes rolled up and he passed out.

'You've killed him,' Rix said, but Butch grinned and shook his head.

'Toss some water over him. I'll bet he'll feel more like tellin' us where to find that key when he comes round.'

Butch was right. The badly hurt man told them and watched with pain-filled eyes as they dragged out the box of explosives, some coils of fuse and a box of detonators.

'Wha — you — doin'?' the wounded man gasped.

'Don't worry about it,' Butch said and shot him through the head.

They took some grub and a part-bottle of whiskey, a few cartons of ammunition, and paused on the way back to their mounts to look up at the mountain.

It was one massive fire now, smoke turning the afternoon into dusk, the sun a pale-grey disc, flames leaping hundreds of feet into the air.

Butch laughed as he tied the box of dynamite behind his saddle.

'Who said Butch Satterlee was dumb?'

Rix didn't answer — but he reckoned his pard was a lot smarter than he'd thought.

Lomas and his men would be too busy fighting the fire to even think about guarding the dam.

⋆ ⋆ ⋆

Corey Lomas was telling the cook what he wanted for supper — he had shot a turkey in the brush earlier and he wanted it roasted with potatoes and carrots and if there weren't any cranberries, he would settle for a sauce made from local blackberries and wild honey.

'And add some of those herbs you used for seasoning that duck I had last week,' Lomas said. He had grown used to good food since he had made some money and was able to hire himself a decent cook. The men had the usual ranch fare but it was cooked and presented more as though they were eating in a restaurant, which likely explained why a lot of men wanted to come work for him. 'And I think I might as well have that . . .'

It was at that juncture that he heard all the yelling in the yard. Irritated, he stepped out on to the porch and saw several of the cowboys who had been working at chores around the home ground, gathered near the corrals and pointing to the south-east.

His blood chilled because he smelled the smoke first and a surge of panic rose up to twist his very guts. *Fire!* the one thing he feared most up here in the hills. Not just because of the danger of its wiping out the ranch but because of the timber that would be destroyed, timber that was now his livelihood — and could be well into the future. As long as it stood, growing free, ready for felling and milling into railroad ties.

He ran into the yard, the men shouting to him and pointing. They didn't need to: it was all too plain to see.

Serpents of flames writhing into a sky that was almost blotted out by the heavy pall of grey-black smoke. They could even hear it way down here, the resinous sap exploding with the heat, shattering trees, hurling blazing branches and slivers far into the brush, starting fresh fires.

'Potluck Ridge, boss!' Long Frank Donahue said unnecessarily, words slurred because of the bandages around his broken nose.

'Kerrr-ist!' Lomas said, his heart pounding now, himself momentarily unable to move or think of anything, hypnotized by the fury of that fire.

'We goin' up there?' asked Baldy Reems, not quite as heavily bandaged as Long Frank; he sounded scared even as he asked the question.

The words jarred Lomas out of his frozen state. He wrenched his gaze away from the fire and drilled a cold stare into the cowboys.

'The hell're you standin' there for? Get mounted! Load the buckboard with digging tools, plenty of sacks and burlap — better throw in some dynamite, too, in case we have to blast a fire-break.'

'Plenty of dynamite at the line camp, boss,' said one of cowboys as he ran towards the barn.

'OK! Just load the other gear and for Chrissakes let's *get up there* before the whole damn mountain goes! Buck, saddle my palomino — No, wait! I ain't riskin' her up there. Make it the claybank with the black ear-tip!'

He ran back into the house, not really knowing why, stood inside the door, trying to think. *Jesus!* What did he want . . . ? His sixgun, rifle, leather chaps, gloves — hell almighty, *move, dammit! Move!*

As he ripped off his jacket and danced about his room trying to pull on the stiff leather chaps over his trousers, another thought came to him and added to his general frantic state:

How the hell did the fire start!

⋆ ⋆ ⋆

They would have seen the fire even down in Keystone by now. Certainly Margarita Ingram had seen it and was busy organizing her six riders, ready to ride.

They all lived in the Black Hills and they were all in danger now: fire was the common enemy and everyone had to fight it, deprive it of a victory that would see total ruin and probably much loss of life if it wasn't stopped in its tracks. *Much easier said than done*, Margarita knew.

But she led her men away from her ranch up on to the dangerous, narrow trails that would take them to Potluck Ridge — wondering who had been stupid enough to start that fire. It had to be Satterlee and Cotton Rix. Casey was out to get Lomas and Judge Bligh, but she didn't think he would go so far as to set the hills ablaze. He knew the consequences, and though she knew he was vengeance-bent, he also knew where to draw the line.

Which, in a way, was unfortunate.

Because Casey didn't know just how much *she* wanted to have Corey Lomas brought to his knees — or the price she was prepared to pay just to see it happen.

* * *

Judge Bligh was busy comforting Lucille who had, naturally enough, been devastated by Waylon Dodge's death, when Hiram Skate the barber brought the news that there was smoke in the hills.

'Black and heavy, Judge,' panted the overweight barber, still holding a razor with drying soapy foam clinging to the blade. 'Can't see no flames yet but it has to be a big'n, that fire . . .'

Bligh patted the sobbing Lucille on

the shoulder, said, 'Excuse me, m'dear', and followed Skate outside on to the porch. The judge stopped in his tracks when he saw the long curling swirl of thick smoke rising above the hills that rose steeply behind the town. He reeled, clutching at his chest.

'My God!' he gasped, face grey.

'She's a beaut, ain't she, Judge?'

Bligh rounded on the wheezing fat man. 'Don't sound so pleased, you blamed fool! Ring the church bell! Mobilize every able-bodied man — except those working in my mill — and get up into the hills and beat back that fire — or it'll wipe us out!' *Wipe him out financially, anyway . . .*

As he spoke, he looked across town to where smoke and steam rose above the buildings from his sawmill. He had thousands sunk into that mill. *Thousands!* The fire had to be stopped before it wiped Keystone off the map. *Had* to be stopped . . .

'Father . . . ?'

He turned at Lucille's voice and saw

her standing in the door of the house, holding a sodden kerchief, eyes red from crying. 'Come back inside . . . '

He caught the sob in her voice and swore softly. All morning he had had her tears and crying and wailing, forcing himself to be sympathetic over the death of a man he had had little time for, anyway. Damned if he was going to sit there all afternoon, too, and listen to the same thing. He had too many things to think about, and that fire was top of the list.

'Go back, Lucille. I'll have one of the womenfolk come over and stay with you.' *God, he felt so — weak!*

He started to stalk away and she called him again and again but he waddled to the front gate and wavered as he opened it, clinging to the frame.

'You'll be all right,' he called and he knew she would, because Lucille might be his daughter, but she was one of those women who could always wheedle her way into folks' goodwill and get all the attention she wanted.

Just like her mother, he thought bitterly, hurrying back towards his office. *Just like her . . .*

* * *

Casey was quite a while getting to Potluck Ridge, having been on the far side of the river, so that he had to ride all the way up to the ford before he could cross. It brought him out on riverbottom land north of the trail up to Potluck.

And on the way he saw Lomas's dam brooding at the end of the old channel, straddling it, like a giant board holding back all that water. Too bad it wasn't higher up the slope, then the headgates could be opened and water released to flood down the slopes and extinguish the fire.

He slowed the paint as he started up towards the ridge, coughing a little in the smoke, ash and sparks raining down upon him and the horse. The paint was leery about approaching the fire, the roar of the flames coming like thunder now, interspersed by the gunshot sounds of exploding trees and saplings. He could hear, mingled with all the other chaos, the whinnying of horses that were much closer to the flames, and the unintelligible shouting of many men.

He saw the line camp cabin off to his left, a frightened mount ground-hitched outside, wrenching at its reins. It was a claybank with a black-tipped ear and he recalled seeing such a horse somewhere. Just as he realized it had been in Lomas's corral the day he had returned something smacked his left arm and knocked him out of the saddle.

The sound of the gunshot was lost in the turmoil of the fire further up the ridge, but even as he hit the ground, he knew it must have come from the cabin.

12

Flood

He rolled and grunted in pain as his weight went on to his left arm, thrust off swiftly and dragged his sixgun out of leather as more bullets churned the grass around him.

Casey slid on his back across the grass, the paint running into the edge of the brush, the other horse still fighting to free itself from the large rock holding its rein-ends to the ground. He saw the rifle barrel at one of the cabin windows, moving as it sought him, paused, and fired.

The bullet passed close and he flopped on to his belly, using his left hand to steady the Colt, noting that it wasn't numbed so maybe the bullet had merely gouged his upper arm and hadn't ploughed into him. Two fast shots sent splinters flying from the window's edge and the rifle barrel disappeared.

'You're wasting time, Corey!' Casey called, replacing the used shells as he spoke. 'You ought to be up there fighting that fire!'

'Rather stay and kill you!' The rifle spoke again and again, four raking shots that had Casey spitting grass and grit as he slid further down the slope. 'You'll be hunted wherever you go now! Remembered as the crazy son of a bitch who set the Black Hills on fire!'

'Not me, Corey. Likely Satterlee and Rix.'

Lomas was silent a moment. 'Could be. But they're your pards, I hear, busted you outta jail.'

'No pards of mine. Tell me, you looking for dynamite in there?'

Again that short silence before Lomas answered. 'So? We need some to blast a firebreak.'

'Did you get it?'

Hesitation. 'No — it's gone, and one

of my men's dead in here!'

'Butch and Rix, for sure. They want to blow your dam.'

A longer period of silence this time. 'You put 'em up to it!'

'Might've mentioned it. Just the headgates, though.'

'Goddamn you, Casey, why couldn't you stay dead!'

'My spirit would never rest until I'd squared things with you, Corey. That's why I want that fire put out. This is all my land that's burning up.'

'The hell it is!' Lomas surprised him by suddenly laughing. 'Man, you think you're ever gonna get back this place! I'd rather see it go up in smoke than let you get your hands on it again!'

'Well, that's what I aim to do, Corey — and leave you dead when I do.'

The rifle suddenly whiplashed and the bullet sang past Casey's ear. But he didn't return the fire.

'Save your lead, Corey. By the time you send somewhere for dynamite it's going to be too late to stop that fire spread.'

'Damn you! You think you can keep me pinned down here while my timber burns up!'

'Reckon I could do it. But I've got a deal for you.'

'What kinda deal?' Lomas sounded sceptical, on the point of laughing in Casey's face again.

Until Casey said,

'I know dynamite, can judge just how much to use — not like Butch and Rix. They'll use all they've got.'

'Judas, there was almost a full box here! They — they'll blow the dam to hell and the whole country down river'll be flooded!'

'So we best not waste any more time. Let's get after them and stop them before they blow the whole dam.'

'Wait a minute — what you got in mind?'

'Stop those two fools, take the dynamite and blast through the side of the old channel. Only take three — four sticks to break through that ridge of dirt, it's all crumbly now. Open your headgates and let loose a few thousand gallons and it'll flood through the new channel we make, fill that hollow at the foot of the ridge to a depth of ten feet or more, and be a lot wider'n that.'

'A ready-made firebreak! But most of the water'll go into the river!'

'Doesn't matter. Won't be enough to do any real damage. Maybe jam up some of those logs you've already got floating down to the mill, that's all . . .'

Silence.

'No more time, Corey! We've got to move *now*! No telling how far ahead those two are.'

'All right. Now you stand up and throw your gun on the ground.'

'Go to hell — you're coming or you're not. But I'm leaving.'

'Goddamnit, Case!'

But Casey ran to where his paint was standing now, staring upslope, concentrating on the fire, and it jumped as he fell against it and grabbed the saddle horn. He swung up easily into the saddle, turned downslope and started to ride away. As he did, the cabin door crashed open and Corey Lomas came out, rifle held low down, at the ready.

The man paused only briefly, then ran for his claybank.

Smoke was writhing about them as they raced along the precarious trail back towards the dam, but higher up the slope than the way Casey had used coming from the river. Lomas kept looking at Casey as they rode, leery, untrusting, one hand riding his sixgun's butt.

There was no sign of Satterlee or Rix, except a couple of fresh-looking places where the edge of the trail had broken away: *in a hurry*, thought Casey and his mouth tightened grimly.

If they didn't catch up with those two idiots he knew they would use too much explosive, shatter the dam wall, if not completely, surely enough to start it cracking and crumbling. The massive amount of water that would be released all at once would extinguish the fire, OK — or form a large fire-break the flames couldn't leap — but it would be the end of the whole of Keystone County. He hated to think how many people could be drowned . . .

Including himself and Lomas.

'There they are!'

Lomas yelled, standing in the stirrups, sliding his Winchester out of his saddle scabbard, even as Casey saw the two outlaws. He felt his belly knot up.

They were riding hell for leather towards them — coming up out of the old riverbed below the dam.

'Jesus! They must've already planted the dynamite!'

Casey yelled it aloud but if Lomas heard he gave no sign. The rifle at his shoulder cracked in three fast shots and that got the attention of Satterlee and Rix. They instinctively hauled rein when they saw the others, Rix throwing a frightened glance over his shoulder.

Hell! thought Casey. *The fuse must be already burning!*

Butch and Rix angled sharply upslope, unshipping their rifles, shooting wildly, not really intending to hit anyone, just intent on getting away from the vicinity of the dam. Lomas had no mind to let them escape now he was this close to them, men who had harassed him and his herds for months.

He skidded his claybank to a halt, slid from the saddle and cursed the horse to a standstill as he laid the rifle across its back, levering and shooting.

Cotton Rix lurched and swayed, dropping his gun, grabbing at the saddle horn. He missed and fell hard, the horse plunging away. Lying there, eyes wide in fear, one clawed hand reaching, he yelled,

'Butch! Butch!'

But Satterlee barely glanced at him, raked with his spurs and urged his own mount on, stretching out close along the horse's back. Lomas was still shooting but his claybank was skittish now and he had to stop and run after it. Casey fired at Butch, lead passing over the outlaw. He lowered his rifle slightly and triggered again.

He missed Satterlee, but his lead struck the horse and it whinnied, half-rearing as it swerved, and Butch was flung almost completely out of the saddle. He clung on desperately, one boot still in the stirrups, as the horse began to go down. He kicked free, hit the slope and started rolling, lashing out with his boots at small rocks and brush, trying to stop his slide. Lomas fired at him as he slid past and then Satterlee managed to halt his progress, wrenched around, sixgun blazing at Casey.

Casey hauled the paint aside and triggered the rifle one-handed, angled down. Satterlee jerked. Casey spun the rifle around the lever, jacking in a fresh load, fired again. Butch slammed over backwards and began a slide down towards the riverbed, loose-limbed, already dead.

Lomas was still trying to get back in the saddle as Casey wheeled the paint and spurred towards the dam.

Suddenly there was a shattering explosion that literally blew him out of the saddle, overturning the paint. Twisting in mid-air, deafened, he saw Lomas flattened to the ground, his claybank rolling across him.

Then there was a glimpse of shattered logs and gouts of earth and rocks, all abruptly blotted out by a colossal column of water, rising out of the dam, climbing rapidly to fill the sky, then tumbling back towards the earth with a monumental roaring thunder that seemed to shake the world itself.

He might have yelled but if he did he had no idea what he said as he saw the massive wave smash into the slope, instantly tearing out trees and rocks, flooding towards them with the speed of a runaway locomotive — and a hundred times as much noise.

It hit with the force of a buffalo in full charge just below them and tore at the slope like some ravenous, living beast, gouging out tons of dirt and boulders as it crushed everything in its path, obliterating the old channel as it poured into the river and spread out in a seething, murky, foaming flood.

And then he felt the mountain give way beneath him and he and the paint were both tumbling down into the accelerating deluge, in the midst of a colossal landslide. Abruptly the world disappeared as he hurtled into oblivion, tumbling, choking, knowing he was going to either drown or be crushed like an insect under a boot.

* * *

Those fighting the fire not only heard the explosion, they *felt* it, the ground trembling beneath their feet, some blazing trees toppling, scattering the people.

Margarita was knocked off her feet and Musty, her wrangler, helped her up, unsteady on his own feet.

'What happened . . . ?'

'An explosion of some sort,' she

answered, surprised that her own voice sounded to her as if she were speaking into an empty barrel. She poked at her ears, watching the others gathering themselves, puzzled by what had happened, the fire still roaring around them. 'Maybe Lomas dropped the dynamite he went after at his line camp . . . '

Maybe there was even a touch of hope in her voice that this had actually happened, but there was no time for an answer as they all turned towards a roaring sound that even overwhelmed the noise of the burning, exploding trees. The ground was quivering under their feet again and smudged, pale faces turned towards each other, sensing some rapidly approaching danger.

'Look!' screamed the wrangler, but was doubtful that anyone heard him, though they did look where he was frantically pointing.

Muddy rivulets of water were spouting into the hollow, rapidly spreading into small streams, the edges moving with such speed and force that the water was already cutting away at the ground.

Margarita's eyes widened and she clutched at her chest as she wrenched her head up towards the now deafening thunder between the ridges . . .

And saw the writhing, muddy, torrent of water, like a living, towering wall, smashing down into the hollow, the level rapidly surging up the slope to where they stood.

Everyone seemed to move at once, breaking for the higher ground — which took them closer to the blazing trees — and still the gushing flood lapped at their heels, tugged at their feet, knocking their legs from under them.

* * *

The sawmill hands working in the holding pool, dragging logs that floated out of the chutes towards the sloping bank, were the first to realize all was not as it should be upstream.

Other men outside the pool, waist-deep in the river, were pulling logs into position with their hooks, reversing their poles and then punching the logs towards the chutes that guided them into the holding pool. One big man — called 'Swede' by everyone although he came from Russia — lifted his arms and said,

''Ey! Dis vater com up to my arm spit!'

Another man lost his footing, swearing as his face went under, and two others stumbled, knocked by suddenly bobbing logs.

'Aw, Mary, Joseph and Jesus!' growled an Irishman suddenly half-wading, half-swimming awkwardly towards the anchored log wall of the holding pool. 'The river's comin' down!' He raised his voice, trying to make himself heard over the thumping sounds of the donkey-engines, the hissing of steam and the endless churning ring of the saws eating wood. '*The river's comin' down! Run . . .'*

It was too late for the Paddy: a rushing surge smashed him into a log and another, hurtling in so fast it made a bow wave, crushed his head like a ripe melon. The others were yelling, struggling, but the surge was too great and a huge wall of tumbling logs from the river rose up and spilled into the holding pool, crushing men and walls, wrecking sheds and benches, scattering piles of sawn ties, dousing the furnace that produced the steam that powered the big saws and conveyor belts. Jets of live steam writhed amongst the men. An engine exploded, shattered metal swirling through the mill like shrapnel from an artillery shell.

The hundreds of logs in the river bunched up and intertwined, locked together in an immovable wall, rearing above the roaring river's level, swaying, tumbling . . .

The water rose at a furious speed, collapsed most of the mill's walls and roofing, and edged up the slope towards the streets of Keystone itself.

Unstoppable.

* * *

Casey couldn't believe he was still alive.

He was half-drowned, retching filthy river-water, coughing, sinking beneath the turbulent surface, rising, snatching a mouthful of air, sinking again — all the time being whipped along by the hurtling current that showed no signs of slackening.

He was far downstream before it eased a little, and he was able to stay mostly on the surface. The water had spread here, inundating the country to either side, now full of trees and bawling or drowned animals, bits of farmhouses from the upper reaches — the Good Lord alone knew where the people were.

He couldn't fight the current, his left arm was hurting now. A quick examination showed he had guessed right earlier: the bullet had gouged a groove in the flesh, but had missed muscle and tendon. He used his arms just enough to keep his head above water as much as possiblc, his body being spun around again and again. Several times he was carried downriver backwards.

He thrust wildly at the root-end of a hickory-tree but one of the snaking limbs caught him across the face, opening a gash. It dazed him and he sank under, lost direction and felt the beginnings of panic instantly grasp him. Which way was up? It was all dark and murky even just a couple of feet under. He thrashed wildly, kicking out with his legs against water that was moving so fast it wanted to stretch his limbs out straight. He swallowed water and began to choke and drown.

He crashed into something, instinctively snatched at it, felt his fingernails gouge into pulpy wood that was soft and slimy, some of the substance breaking away. His second grab was better and his arm slid half-way round the trunk of a sapling. He clung desperately, wrenching his head out of the water and gulping air that seared his lungs.

Eyes stinging he flung wet hair back and blinked. Corey Lomas was clinging to a tree not three yards away, a deep gash showing on his forehead. He kind of hung there and Casey was pretty sure he was unconscious or close to it. The man began to slide off into the river and Casey — hesitating briefly, cursing — changed grip, thrust himself away from his own tree. He had to dive under Lomas's tree and when he surfaced, was just in time to catch the sinking Corey by the jacket. He hung on with aching fingers, let Corey's abandoned log come down upon them and then awkwardly got his free arm across it.

They travelled half a mile downriver before he was able to drag Lomas's body close in against the log, sink down under the man and then surge up, lifting him half across at waist-level. Near exhaustion, he clung there, using one arm to hold Lomas in position, as the log spun end-for-end, rolled a little, which meant more grabbing and sinking and near-drowning. Then when at last he had them both back into a riding position, the damn log would begin to roll again and he would have to start over.

Everything was a blur. He reckoned they would be down at the town in half an hour at this rate — if there was any town left. He lifted a heavy head to look up at the sky. Still lots of smoke hanging up there, dimming the sun. They were round the bend now so he was unable to see if the fire was still burning.

Then, partly dreaming with encroaching exhaustion, partly beginning to think about how they were going to get ashore without being killed by all the floating debris, he heard a growling sound and suddenly there was a heavy weight on his back, something wrapping around his neck, trying to pull him free of the log.

It took only seconds to realize what it was: one of Lomas's arms! The man had come to, edged along the log and flung himself on to Casey, trying to wrench him free.

Casey was taken by surprise and had trouble hanging on, his grip beginning to loosen. Lomas had one leg hooked over the log, was kicking at him with the other, at the same time trying to throttle him.

'You — crazy — sonuver — ' Casey gasped. 'We'll both — drown!'

'No — just you! Never be a better — chance to get — rid of you! Drowned in — the flood!'

Casey fought to hang on, worked one arm free, threw an awkward punch at Lomas's face.

'I should've — let you — go when you — slipped off that log!'

'Then you — had your — chance and missed it!' Lomas heaved up with the last word, drove a knee into Casey's kidneys. The man gagged and started to slip. Lomas renewed his efforts to overwhelm him.

He kicked savagely but the blows were slowed and softened by the water, though they still hurt Casey's belly. Lomas drove an elbow against his head and Casey saw fireworks, felt his hand sliding over the slippery surface. Corey Lomas sensed or felt that he had loosened Casey's hold and bared his teeth, chopping at the other's neck.

Casey pulled his head aside, snapped it back into Lomas's face, opening the gash in the man's forehead even more. Blood flowed and blinded Lomas and in desperation he drew back one leg and snapped it out straight — just as Casey was knocked off the log by a sweeping branch. The boot caught him in the face and he went under, rolled over and over by the raging water, bobbing up yards away, submerging again, and although the panting Lomas waited, he did not see the body surface.

'Son of a bitch!' he gasped with feeling, dousing his face in the river to wash the blood from his eyes. 'That's the end of you!'

When he could see again, he realized he was coming into the last bend of the river and that the town lay just beyond. Time to think about how he would get ashore.

Then he saw the huge log-jam stretching across the river, a ready-made bridge to safety. As he was borne down towards the wall of logs that would stop his tree — and all the other debris behind him — he noticed that the sawmill was mostly gone, just shattered timbers and one donkey-engine's smokestack leaning at a crazy angle above the surface of muddy water that stretched up into the town itself — though not as far as he might have thought, lapping at the buildings.

There were men clambering over the jammed logs, making their way back towards the shallows where milled timber floated amidst doors and planks and an occasional body. Had to admire those lumberjacks, sure-footed as monkeys the way they raced over those wet, splintered logs. In one hell of a hurry, too . . .

He saw someone point in his direction and he lifted one arm, waving.

'I could use some help!' he called, pointing to the logs and some floaters that nudged the tangled wall of the main jam. 'Gimme a hand!'

They didn't seem to hear — or, rather, they didn't understand his words, apparently. Just as he couldn't quite make out what they were shouting, waving him off frantically.

Off? Like hell! He was coming in!

He clambered up so he was half-lying along the tree, ignoring the men on shore now, who were running away, splashing through the shallows, high-tailing it up the flooded street, well away from the mill.

'What the hell . . . ? Hey! Gimme a hand, damnit!'

Then two words reached him clearly when he was only a couple of yards from the log-jam and he prepared to leap,

‘. . . gonna — blow!’

Frowning, he raised his head, didn’t feel any wind blowing. Then he started to scream but it was too late. He saw the smoking wisps of burning fuses in amongst the logs and knew now what the man had meant when he said it was going to *blow* . . .

They were using dynamite to loosen the log-jam and so allow the banked-up water to flow away freely, downstream, away from the town, draining the streets before the whole town was flooded.

He threw himself into the water, striking out wildly with thrashing strokes that were so uncoordinated that he didn’t actually move an inch.

And then the dynamite blew.

Expertly placed by men who were used to freeing log-jams, the explosive erupted in a series of flash-fast detonations, lifting the logs in a humping, rippling wave, unlocking the entanglement, the blast heaving them skywards, freeing them, shattering some into splinters, sending huge fountains of muddy water and chunks of the riverbottom dozens of feet into the air.

The surge of the banked-up water started almost immediately and hundreds of loosened logs slid away from the shattered holding pool, caught by the current and carried away from the town by the Big Bad River.

Whatever was left of Corey Lomas went with them.

* * *

It was dark when Casey staggered into the camp in the hills where the surviving firefighters were cooking supper, recuperating from their ordeal.

Two men led him in, half-carrying him, and he saw Margarita Ingram rise from her place around the cooking-fire and limp across. She had one arm in a sling.

'We thought you were dead.'

It was said expressionlessly. He couldn't tell if she was glad to see him or not. Someone pressed a mug of hot coffee into his hands and he took it gratefully.

'No thanks to Corey Lomas.' Casey sat down on a log.

'Don't worry about him,' the girl told him. 'He's gone. Caught in the log-jam off Keystone as they were blasting it free. Or so we hear.'

Casey snapped his head up. 'The town survived?'

She nodded. 'Those lumberjacks knew what to do. They blew the log-jam, which allowed the banked-up waters to flow past. Oh, about a quarter of Keystone was flooded and some people were drowned, but it wasn't the catastrophe everyone feared. Bligh had a heart attack. We're not sure of all the details yet.'

Casey told them about Butch Satterlee and Rix blowing the dam, using too much explosive.

'Well, they did us a favour — the water filled the hollow between the ridges here, and the fire couldn't jump across. It burned itself out. Most of the timber's useless, though. I suppose you'll be taking over your land again?'

Casey didn't answer, sipped more coffee and took a piece of cornpone and bacon offered by the weary wife of one of the other ranchers. He chewed, the girl watching. Then he said:

'Hey, is that my paint, yonder . . . ?'

She turned to look at the small remuda in a crude corral made by rope stretched between some of the standing saplings.

'Yes. He wandered in a little while ago. Seems mostly all right but one leg is strained and he's lost a little hide.'

Casey stood and limped across to the horse which seemed glad to see him. He stroked its muzzle, examined it by firelight. Yes, one leg would have to be rested and those cuts could stand some treatment, one needing a few stitches.

'You can bring him to my place, it's still mostly in one piece. Leave him to recover there,' the girl offered.

He nodded his thanks, glanced at her

and saw her stiffen a little at his look.

'What is it?' she asked warily.

'You're real glad Lomas is dead, huh?'

'Aren't you? Everyone here is.'

'But none as glad as you.'

'What are you getting at?'

'Rix was a nervous nelly, talked a lot to keep himself calmed down. Mentioned once that you hated Corey Lomas more'n anyone else in the Black Hills. I wondered why.'

She said nothing, just stared at him. 'He said that about six months ago you suggested to Lomas that you and he should amalgamate your spreads, seal the deal with — marriage.'

'I — didn't know what he was really like then. I — I wanted *security*, Casey! I'm nearly thirty and . . . '

He waited but although her eyes narrowed she didn't continue.

'But he laughed at you,' he suggested. 'Said even if your spread wasn't too small and useless to him, he still wouldn't marry you. I think he meant only that he wasn't the marrying kind but you took the hurt to heart.'

'And why not?' she hissed. 'He humiliated me! In front of his men. I knew I wasn't strong enough to fight a man like Lomas alone so when Butch and Rix were run off I saw a chance to use them to get back at him. But they were too stupid, afraid to make any real move, scared of Durango.'

'Then I came along, with a real reason to want Lomas dead. So you used me.'

'Well?' Some defiance there. 'I *had* to.'

'I guess that's how you saw it, but I don't like it. I remember that time you said when I joined Butch and Rix, 'Don't spoil it for me, Casey!' You meant: don't spoil your chance to nail Lomas, didn't you?'

She tossed her head. 'Well, he's dead now and I'm glad. I'll try to make it up to you while you're getting your land together again.' She placed her hand on his arm, looking up into his weary, battered face. 'I mean that, Casey.'

'I think you do. But I won't be staying.'

'What . . . ?' She was incredulous.

'Be years before that land's any good for cattle again.' He turned to pat the paint. 'Meantime, I'll take you up on your offer to rest up my horse on your place.'

'Then?' she asked tautly.

'Then I reckon I'll ride north to a certain Indian tribe's winter camp. With luck, I'll be there in time for the birth of my son.'

'He'll be a half-breed!' Disapproving now.

'He'll be my *son*. I want to see him grow up — with me and his mother.'

'My God, you're nothing but a squaw man!' She sounded disgusted. 'Why, for a moment there I thought we might even . . . ' She broke off when she saw his bleak eyes.

'No,' he said flatly and walked past her to the log by the fire, sat down and picked up his coffee-mug.

Striding away angrily into the shadows, she snapped, 'Find somewhere else to rest your damn Indian horse.'

THE END